THE NEW SHINING WHITE MURDER

Death by drowning — in a bubble bath. The cleanest murder ever! That is the fate of a leading advertising executive shortly after having engaged the services of Adam Flute, Private Investigator. Lured to the scene of the crime, Flute gets trapped in a room with the body and only just manages to escape before the police arrive. Despite a starry-eyed blonde secretary, a sultry television actress and the victim's beautiful wife, Flute does finally manage to clear up the mystery.

DREW LAUNAY

THE NEW SHINING WHITE MURDER

Complete and Unabridged

LINFORD
Leicester

First published in Great Britain in 1962
under the name of 'Droo Launay'

First Linford Edition
published 2001

British Library CIP Data

Launay, Droo, *1930* –
   The new shining white murder.
   —Large print ed.—
   Linford mystery library
   1. Detective and mystery stories
   2. Large type books
   I. Title
   823.9'14 [F]

   ISBN 0–7089–5944–X

Published by
F. A. Thorpe (Publishing)
Anstey, Leicestershire

Set by Words & Graphics Ltd.
Anstey, Leicestershire
Printed and bound in Great Britain by
T. J. International Ltd., Padstow, Cornwall

This book is printed on acid-free paper

1

The man's body was lying full length on the stone floor and a twelve-inch arrow was sticking out of his back. It was a clean way of killing someone but a way that needed precision and marksmanship. There was no doubt in my mind that the murderer was handy with a bow.

Uncle Leopold stared at the victim for some time facing the problem which had to be solved quickly. He was in an ugly mood and the bright white light shining in his face made him look pretty sinister.

'Well?' he said, turning to me. 'Who do you think killed him?'

'Well,' said I. 'Probably Robin Hood.'

The argument that might have followed was nipped in the bud by the telephone ringing. I stretched out my shoeless foot, turned down the sound on the television set with my toes and picked up the receiver.

'Adam Flute, Public Relations,' I

yawned into the instrument.

Her voice was sweet, soft as candy floss and she sounded as innocent as de Sade's secretary.

'We're in terrible trouble and need your help,' she said breathlessly. 'Could you possibly come over to Studio 4. We'll explain everything when you get there.'

She hung up before I could ask her name, and I replaced the receiver in its white cradle.

'Who was it?' my uncle asked.

In silence Robin Hood had proved his innocence and was hitting the Sheriff of Nottingham on the head.

'Someone from the Advertising Agency.'

'On Saturday afternoon? They're keeping you busy!'

Slowly I got up off the low sofa and walked over to the window to look at the cold damp November weather. Since I had joined my uncle as an assistant Private Investigator he had virtually retired. While he lived in some draughty country house, I ran the business from his flat, a six roomed affair on the top floor of Porchester Court, a block in the

Bayswater Road overlooking Hyde Park. It was pleasant, discreet, central, and I didn't pay the rent.

I looked at his onion shape as he sat on the very edge of the sofa paralysed by the silent story developing before his eyes, and wondered why he had bothered to come up to London at all.

Robin Hood rode off into the forest and a man in a white overall came on to warn me about my decaying hair roots.

'What would you like to do now?' I asked looking at the programmes. 'There's 'Bossie Bessie of Bluebell Farm', 'Gardening for the Under Twenties' or would you like a game of solitaire?'

'I'd like a brandy.'

As I poured out two mean measures of the pale amber liquid into the pint-sized tumblers at hand, the telephone rang again.

This time it was an older voice, about sixty years older and laced with gin. It rang me up regularly twice a week to complain about the lack of men in the world.

Uncle Leopold was about to start snoring so I patted him on the head and handed him the receiver.

'It's for you.'

I didn't stay to hear what was being said, but sauntered into my bedroom with an idea about getting dressed.

I let my electric shaver battle with my chin for a few minutes, dipped my head in cold water and examined the result. If I had lost some of my boyish complexion, now that I was hitting the middle thirties, I had at least acquired the glazed look of an adult who had lived well. My hair was an indefinite colour but my eyes were brown and pretty fascinating. I had a good jaw, which people liked hitting, and a fair amount of muscle here and there. On the whole I wasn't bad.

I put on a clean crisp white shirt and tried hard to remember where I had heard Miss Soft Voice before. I had only been working for this Advertising Agency a week and could hardly be expected to know everyone. The Managing Director, a pleasant enough organization man, had engaged me to investigate the leakage of the agency's original creative ideas to a rival firm. I had joined the staff as a PR man which automatically exempted me from knowing anything about the business.

In the sitting room Uncle Leo was lying full length on the sofa whispering into the telephone receiver. I slipped out of the flat discreetly and crossed my fingers. With luck he might find himself involved for the next few weeks.

*　*　*

The new office block in Park Lane was full of surprises. The main entrance was in the front, there was a main hall, a sleeping hall porter behind a desk and a couple of automatic lifts that stopped on the floor you wanted if you pressed the right button.

I got into one of the aluminium cages and watched the dial go round to three. When the doors opened I stepped out onto a highly polished parquet floor and made for the gilt-framed, red-lacquered door opposite the lifts which bore the simple legend:

BEDLINGTON, LARDVIK
ADVERTISING LTD.

I walked in and hit a cloud of heavy scent. The corridor straight ahead was thickly carpeted with mustard coloured Wilton and apart from a bright light, coming through a glass panelled office half way down on the right, the rest of the place was in darkness.

I walked towards the light and opened the door. The office was untidy with papers, filing cabinets and an abundance of display showcards begging me to buy air sickness pills and a new pudding mix. No one was hiding under the desk.

I walked further along the corridor and turned left. Round the corner the style changed and the glass panelling gave way to brocade papered walls and satinwood doors. One of these doors had 'Studio 4' in brass well screwed into it.

I tried the handle and opened the door. The room was pretty big. It was painted white, had a ceiling riveted with spot-lights, some expensive photographic equipment lying idle and in the centre a pink marble bath studded with gold stars.

This bath was the attraction of the day. All the lights, about fifty of them, were trained on it and a camera in one corner was focussed in its direction. I guessed that this was the agency's experimental photographic studio, which I had heard people boasting about, and that the bath was under contract.

There didn't seem to be anybody about so I walked up to the bath and took a closer look. Frothing five inches above the top was a shining white foam of bubbles. They made a soft sighing noise as they burst and I had an urge to take a handful and blow them across the room — but I resisted.

A yard or so behind the bath, in small two feet tall letters, someone had left a message for me. It read:

'CHAMBLE'
THE NEW SHINING WHITE TOILET POWDER THAT BUBBLES LIKE CHAMPAGNE

Feel the carbon dioxide lift the dirt right out of your pores.

This made the urge to take a handful of bubbles quite uncontrollable. Drawing up my sleeve I gently dipped my hand into the new shining white foam and felt something soft and flabby underneath.

For a few seconds I let my fingers explore the unexpected mass under the water, then I felt a shape which seemed familiar.

I drew it out of the foam and looked at it. It was pale and hairy and very clean. It belonged to the man who was lying cold and wet under the few inches of bubbles.

After examining it, I let the stiff dead hand drop back with a plop into the water and turned round just in time to see the door close. Someone was locking me in.

2

The photographic studio had no windows, just four walls, the door and a dead man having a bath. The fact that I had been tricked into being locked in the room worried me a little. It was now reasonable to suspect that someone in the agency had tumbled to it that I was not a simple PR man but a Private Eye. Detectives of my calibre were wonderful scapegoats and could be relied on to delay the police in their investigations. I could just imagine the fun I was going to have during the next twenty-four hours trying to convince Scotland Yard that I knew absolutely nothing about the murder.

Before attempting to break down the door and making a bid for freedom, I decided to have a good long look at my new-found friend. I swept the froth of bubbles onto the floor and looked down into the clear pink water at the middle aged man who had stopped breathing the moment a polythene bag had been slipped over his head.

I didn't see the bag at first but when I tried to feel how cold he was, I noticed it. There was a message printed on it telling me to 'TRY CHAMBLE — A LAUGH WITH EVERY BATH.'

He was wearing a drip dry shirt, trousers, a pair of socks, but nothing else. I had only seen him once before, on the day he had come to the flat to engage me.

In one of his trouser pockets I found a key ring and a damp handkerchief. On the small finger of his left hand he wore a pleasantly expensive gold and bloodstone signet ring with some horned animal engraved in the centre.

Satisfied that there was no more to be gained by frisking the soggy corpse, I let him go and stepped back as he first sank, then rose in the pink water, sending waves of lovely bubbles splashing all over the floor.

Using his wet handkerchief I carefully wiped round the edge of the bath to remove any of my fingerprints and turned my attention to the door.

Breaking it down didn't prove as simple as I had imagined, but after unscrewing the lock surround with my pocket knife, losing my temper with the handle and cutting my thumb, I managed to get out.

One of his keys, I felt sure, would fit his office door, so I moved quickly down the corridor and stopped outside another red lacquered affair bearing the name 'Henry Bedlington' in discreet yellow plastic.

Inside it was very homely. There was a large half moon desk in front of a CinemaScope shaped window which was protected by a venetian blind. The carpet was orange, the walls panelled in white satinwood, there was a built-in television set and tape recorder, a number of golfing cups and a sweet photograph of the dead man himself astride a polo pony.

Another photograph, of a pretty girl, told me that he was married and that his bride was old enough to be his daughter.

He had his own address conveniently written down in his address book, in case he forgot it, and under the heading 'Private Detective' I found mine. This little indiscretion could explain why someone knew more about me than I wished them to.

Cautious by nature, I lifted up the venetian blind to see if the office was overlooked at all, and found myself staring down at the one-way traffic racing along Park Lane.

I was interested to see two police cars drawing up outside the office block and a number of uniformed gentlemen getting out of them and coming into the building. It was plain that whoever had locked me in the studio had also kindly informed the police of my presence.

My instinct told me it was time I got out, so I switched off all the lights and left the office. My best bet was for me to get back to the flat as quickly as possible and wait patiently for events to develop.

Instead of using the lifts I started down the stairs and paused on the first floor to listen to the voices in the entrance hall below. The hall porter had his duties to perform and insisted on searching the building with the police. This suited me admirably as it left the coast reasonably clear.

I waited till the dial above the lift doors indicated the third floor, then went down the stairs and out of the building.

Outside I smiled at the two policemen standing by the cars and hailed a taxi.

Kitty, the Porchester Court telephone operator, was one of the most efficient information services in London. Imprisoned behind a thick glass panel in a small room four feet square, she had a VHF radio set hidden under the switchboard and was illegally tuned in all day to the Police Motor Patrol in the Metropolitan area. She knew about every accident, every disturbance, and every case of indecent exposure before anyone else.

'There are two men behaving suspiciously outside the vicarage in West Hampstead,' she said as I slid the glass panel aside and asked her what messages there were. 'And someone's made an improper suggestion to a woman of fifty-five outside Earls Court tube station.'

The fact that no one would ever make

an improper suggestion to Kitty had never entered her head.

Upstairs in the flat I found a message from Uncle Leo. Owing to unexpected circumstances he had been called away on business and might not be back for a few days. I tore the message up, helped myself to a liberal dose of whisky and ran myself a bath.

I didn't stay in the water long. It was the first bath I hadn't enjoyed for years, a question of association of ideas. I idled into the sitting room, sat down in front of the fire and played around with a few crazy notions for a couple of hours. Someone had tried to play a very nasty trick on me and I couldn't just let it go. But after working on the facts I knew, I decided to wait for further developments. I didn't wait long, the telephone rang as I leaned over to switch on the television.

Her voice was young, warm and calm. She told me her name was Ninette Bedlington and that she would like to see me as soon as possible. I finished my drink in one gulp, lit a cigarette and padded into the bedroom to change.

Someone somewhere was too fond of using my name.

⋆　⋆　⋆

The house was modern, square and probably had fifteen bedrooms. The area was Primrose Hill where it wouldn't harm you to have a good expense account.

The small drive had a wall round it with wrought iron gates which were closed. I left the car parked outside and walked up the gravelled driveway. The setting was clean and safe and lifeless, the red bricks of the house were really red brick and the front steps had been scrubbed daily since they had been laid. I stood under the cold white porch light and pressed the bell on the left side of the thick polished oak door.

She managed to be five feet tall, had black bobbed hair, alarmingly innocent eyes, a beautiful little mouth and a figure that belonged to a sixteen year old.

'Come in,' she whispered.

I followed her through to the drawing room which was furnished exactly like

Bedlington's office. The panelling, the books, the built-in television set, orange carpets and venetian blinds were all the same. Most of the ornaments were identical and so were the light fittings. I wondered where the man managed to get so much imagination.

I let myself sink back in a black sofa and accepted the idea of a drink.

Ninette Bedlington was wearing a coffee-coloured dress with a few hundred pounds' worth of gold trinkets round her small neck and wrists. Her shoes were of brown crocodile and her short cigarette holder was real tortoise shell. No one was missing out on anything.

'What's the trouble?' I asked as she handed me a dry martini.

'My husband,' she said.

'What about him?'

'I haven't seen him for a week.'

'And what do you want me to do about it?'

'I'd like you to find him.'

I looked at the diamond ring on her finger, slightly smaller than a half-crown, and wondered whether Bedlington had made a will in her favour.

'Have you any idea where he might be?' I was going to play it cold and clinical for a while. I didn't believe in coincidences.

'No.'

'You think another woman is involved?'

'Possibly.'

I had dealt with so many broken marriages that the routine questions came out automatically.

'Do you care?'

She looked up and gave me the once over. She was very alive and not stupid.

'In a way,' she said at last.

'In what way?'

'If my husband *has* deserted me I'd like to know. I wouldn't mind a divorce.'

She offered me a cigarette and leaned forward to light it for me. I held her unsteady little hand for a moment and the contact made her blush. She was really very young and badly in need of protection.

'I'm an actress,' she said suddenly without being asked, 'and I would like to go back to the stage. My husband stopped me going on with my career when we got married.'

'Why?'

'He's in advertising and doesn't like the publicity.'

I leaned back and hoped that someone else would try to figure that one out. But she was sweet to look at and I was beginning to enjoy the interview.

'Why did you ring me?' I asked. 'There are hundreds of detective agencies in London.'

Without replying she got up, went to the desk and brought back a small book. It was an address book just like I had seen in Bedlington's own desk. Under the letter P — for Private Detective — was my name again.

'He's had your name for some time now and I know that you're working at the agency for him. I thought you would be the best placed man.'

It was all possible but there was something in her eyes which told me there was more to it than she cared to tell me at present. I was going to be patient, I wasn't in any danger.

She looked up, smiled a nervous little

smile and walked back to the desk to replace the address book. I was about to ask her a few pertinent questions when the front door bell rang.

Instinctively she looked at the clock above the fireplace and raised an eyebrow; it was just past seven, maybe someone was coming to dinner. She didn't move and I got the feeling that maybe she was afraid, or at least wanted me to think so.

'Shall I go?' I asked gallantly.

Ninette nodded nervously. I got up and went into the hall and looked back to see her light a cigarette. All I had to do was step well back when I opened the door so that the shot, if that was the way they were going to kill me, missed.

I didn't give myself time to work things out or ask any questions, but flicked back the mortice lock, pressed myself against the right hand wall and pulled the door open.

On the front doorstep a policeman stood beside a tall thin man whose name was Chaucer, but he didn't know I knew. Chaucer was a detective sergeant who loved his work. For the first time I had to admit I was pleased to see him.

'Yes?' I said politely.

'Is Mrs. Bedlington in?'

'Who shall I say?'

'The police.'

I smiled a smile reserved for such occasions and sauntered back into the drawing room.

'The police,' I said.

Ninette didn't do too badly. She half rose from the sofa, uttered a surprised 'Oh!' and sat down again.

I showed them in and watched how the uniformed gentleman took off his helmet. They have a special helmet-taking-off class at Hendon.

'Mrs. Bedlington?' said Chaucer bowing and scraping, 'Chief Detective Inspector Bowels sent me. I am Detective Sergeant Frank Chaucer.'

'Oh,' said little Ninette again. 'Do please sit down.'

Chaucer did not sit down but swallowed hard to make it quite clear that what he was about to say was going to be very unpleasant.

'I'm afraid I have bad news for you, Mrs. Bedlington,' he started, only just controlling a leer from forming on his thin lips. 'Your husband has been found dead.'

Ninette stood up. From nowhere a tiny handkerchief appeared and too soon she started dabbing at her bone dry eyes. It dawned on me why her husband had got her off the stage.

'He was suffocated then drowned,' Chaucer went on mercilessly, 'and I'm afraid that foul play cannot be ruled out.'

Before he could go on to describe the colour of the victim, Ninette wandered off into a corner sniffing away. It really wasn't a good act, but it had to do. I felt I should move in so I went up behind her and placed a hand on her shoulder.

Through her thin silk shirt I could feel the warmth of her young body. I squeezed her a little and hoped I didn't make it too obvious that I was delighted her husband wouldn't be around for a while.

'I'd like to ask you a few questions, Mrs. Bedlington, if I may,' Chaucer said, coming forward and interrupting my little moment of pleasure.

'Yes, yes of course.' She had dried her dry eyes by now and could face him bravely.

'But may I first ask who you are, sir?'

He was addressing me as though he didn't want me around.

'I'm sorry,' Ninette said, 'I should have introduced you. This is Mr. Flute, a friend of my husband.'

Chaucer made a note of the name and then turned to Ninette.

'How long had you been married, Mrs. Bedlington?'

'Just over two years.'

'Did your husband have many enemies?'

'He was in advertising.'

'Is there anyone you might suspect?'

'No. No one.'

He wasn't getting anywhere and knew it. No doubt he was hoping for some lead which might get him a promotion in ten years' time.

After a moment of embarrassed silence, Chaucer made an ungracious exit after requesting Ninette to call at the morgue to identify her husband.

At the door he assured me that a car would call for Mrs. Bedlington in the morning and that Scotland Yard would do their best to find the criminal as soon as possible.

As far as I was concerned Ninette's demure and innocent act was over and when I went back into the dining room I didn't soften the tone of my voice.

'You knew he was dead of course?' I asked.

'No.' She seemed astonished by my question and I was surprised to see the glint of a tear in one of her eyes.

'You didn't?'

'No, of course not!'

Her lower lip was trembling and she was having difficulty in pouring herself out a steadying drink.

'It's a bit of coincidence that you should call me to-night though, isn't it?'

'I suppose so.' She was swallowing a large gin and water without any trouble and it seemed to do her nerves good.

'What made you ring me up to-night and not ... this afternoon, or this morning, or even yesterday?'

She crossed the room swiftly, opened the drawer of the desk and brought out a long brown envelope.

'This was put through the letter box just about an hour ago. I rang you up as soon as I had opened it.'

I took the envelope, shook out a thickly folded piece of tissue paper, unwrapped it, and stared at the gold and bloodstone signet ring that fell into the palm of my hand.

3

'It's a ring,' I said examining the ring carefully, the small red spots of the dark green bloodstone, the engraved horned animal, the size of the aperture.

'Haven't you seen it before?' Ninette asked.

'No.'

'My husband wore it on the little finger of his left hand.'

I looked up and met her gaze. There was nothing in it that gave anything away and it was just possible that she didn't know I had spent a few happy minutes giving her old man a bath.

'I only met him once, you know,' I said calmly.

'But wasn't he wearing the ring then?'

'Maybe.'

'When I rang you up I thought the ring had been sent to me by one of his girl friends — as a sort of dig. He had the irritating habit of lending it to anyone he might be . . . admiring.'

She helped herself to a second large gin, with a drop of water and a squirt of lemon. The news that she was a widow was taking its time to sink in, and it didn't seem to be a depressing process.

'What were you going to ask me to do?' I asked.

'Find out who the girl friend was.'

'Then it seems that I am now redundant.'

'Why? I'll need you more than ever!'

I toyed with that phrase for some time and gave her a long steady look.

'To do what?'

'Find out who killed Henry.'

As she went back to the sofa to sit in one corner with her lovely legs tucked under her, I ambled across to the cocktail cabinet and gave myself another drink. From where I stood I could see down the front of her dress, a not unpleasant pastime.

'That sort of detection is best left to the police, you know,' I said.

She turned round. Either she knew

what I was up to or she was interested in my face.

'The police will take ages! And they'll only turn up a lot of dirt which is best left alone.'

'Well I can't really investigate a murder officially.'

'But unofficially? I could always increase the salary Henry was paying you, you would still be working on his instructions.'

She was taking off her heavy gold necklace and I was thinking of her inheritance.

'Not a bad idea,' I said. 'No one could object.'

She, of course, had no idea of my limitations and obviously had something to hide from the police; I, on the other hand, wouldn't be able to sleep peacefully till I had found out who had locked me in the studio. I had managed to sting dear Henry for thirty-five quid a week, I could always double it.

'Julius Lardvik will be here any minute,' Ninette said suddenly looking up at the clock, 'I'll ask him what he thinks of the idea. If you could find a suspect before the police — it might save a lot of embarrassment all round.'

'Is it wise to bring in Mr. Lardvik?' I asked with due respect to Henry's partner. 'The fewer people in the know, the better.'

'He's my godfather and I like to consult him.'

That piece of information answered a number of questions I had roaming about at the back of my mind. Bedlington and Lardvik were partners and Bedlington had married Lardvik's goddaughter.

'You realize, of course, that *I'll* have to turn up a lot of the dirt?' I said.

'Yes, but you'll keep it all to yourself and not repeat it to the press.'

My price went up a little as I sipped the dry martini. Though I hated the stuff I had to admit it had status. If I drank it, it proved I had tough guts — to me anyway.

'Have you any idea who might have wanted to kill your husband?' I asked, getting down to business.

'Not really. I don't suppose he had many friends. He was a little ruthless.'

I was sticking the end of my thumbnail between my front teeth and leaning heavily on the back of the sofa so that I could be nearer to her and inhale that invigorating scent. I looked pretty pensive and was even thinking.

'Do you know anything about the agency?'

'I have a substantial amount of shares.'

'But did your husband keep you informed about what was going on?'

'Sometimes. He told me he had engaged you.'

'Significant.'

It was a good word. I had used it once by mistake during a Public Relations conference earlier in the week and had been tabbed a bright boy because of it.

'Significant,' I repeated and stroked the stubble on my chin. I was beginning to impress her.

The front door bell rang suddenly and made little Ninette jump a mile. I just went on stroking my chin calmly, after three martinis I was always relaxed.

'Your godfather?'

'Yes, probably.'

I sauntered to the hall and pulled the front door open.

Lardvik and I had never met officially, but we both knew each other by sight. I greeted him with a smile but he couldn't quite reciprocate.

'What are you doing here?' he asked as though vexed by my presence.

He was wearing a royal blue bow tie to match his eyes, a curling beard and a shock of blond hair. He was about forty-five, close to, and very healthy. He had a white shirt, white teeth, a dark suit and a camel hair coat. He also wore a wide brimmed hat on the back of his head to show he was a proud Scandinavian, or some such other arrogant foreigner.

'Do come in. Your goddaughter is waiting for you.'

He abruptly strode into the drawing room to remind me that he was my employer, and I closed the front door humbly behind him, as a servant should. All I knew about Julius Lardvik was that he was the main creative force in the agency. The artist, the ideas man, the genius. Or so he told everyone.

'Darling!' Ninette started, then checked herself remembering I was around. 'You have met Adam Flute?'

'Yes,' Lardvik said, but with disappointing enthusiasm.

'I called him before I knew.'

'Knew what?'

'About Henry.'

'You know about Henry?' Lardvik seemed surprised.

'The police came here a few minutes ago with the news, but we have no details,' I said.

'He was found in the photographic studio, drowned in the Chamble bath,' Lardvik said looking away. He was concerned by the fate of his colleague.

I watched him and Ninette closely, it seemed to be a difficult situation for both of them with a stranger present. Something told me that their relationship was part of the dirt that wasn't to get into the papers.

'Frankly I can't say I'm surprised,' Lardvik added, I felt for my benefit, 'though I wouldn't have thought he'd have the guts to commit suicide.'

I said nothing, nor did Ninette. Scandinavians always had suicide on the brain so maybe that explained that remark. I waited patiently for the conversation to develop.

While Ninette mixed him some unfashionable cocktail, she started explaining my presence. Lardvik sat down on the edge of the armchair and looked between his knees at the carpet. He didn't listen to what she was saying but worked out what the death of his partner would mean to him. Occasionally he mumbled a 'yes' just to give her the impression he was listening, but I knew he wasn't. Henry Bedlington's death was going to complicate his life.

'Don't you think it would be the right thing to do?' Ninette handed him his cocktail and sat down next to him on the armchair.

'Yes. Yes indeed.'

'I suggest that if I moved into Mr. Bedlington's office on Monday and told the staff that I was dealing with the press regarding the tragedy, it would enable me to be at the centre of things,' I said.

He was coming out of it now, his deep trance, he was coming out of it slowly and beginning to realize that he had committed himself to something he didn't want.

'What's wrong with your present room?' he asked trying to find a lead.

'I share it with two other people and there's only one telephone.'

'Oh.'

'I really think it's the best place, Mr. Lardvik. From Bedlington's office I can talk to the reporters on an authoritative basis and see to it that they don't disturb the running of the agency. And we don't want to lose the Chamble account because of badly handled publicity, do we?'

I wasn't giving him a chance to think and as I was standing in front of the fire I was in a more commanding position.

As an artist of sorts Lardvik allowed himself a certain vagueness of character which in this instant permitted him to ask Ninette to repeat what she had already said without causing anyone any particular irritation.

I wasn't so much interested in the way he reacted to the news that she had received Henry's ring anonymously, but by the way he paled when she told him that I wasn't really a member of the staff or a Public Relations Officer but a private detective hired by Bedlington. He was shocked and didn't try to hide it. He couldn't understand why his partner had requested my services behind his back, and I wasn't going to explain anything to him. The simple fact was that Bedlington hadn't trusted anyone of his staff, least of all his closest colleague.

Before anyone could have a change of heart, I finished my drink and made to leave. At the front door Ninette put out her hand for me to shake. I took it and held it for longer than necessary without her objecting. I also stared into her lovely olive-shaped eyes and gave her one of my charming smiles. She didn't mind.

'I'll keep in touch,' I said, 'and please let me know of any new developments.'

She looked at me for a while longer, still holding my sticky hand, then said, 'He didn't seem too pleased about you nosing around, did he? Is that significant?'

She let go of my hand, I stepped back out of the house and watched the door close slowly. I wouldn't have minded knowing why she had really hired me. She was beautiful, she was attractive, she had a lovely little figure, but I didn't trust her a bit.

*   *   *

I spent most of Sunday asleep and undisturbed. Three of the papers had a small paragraph about Henry Bedlington, Agency Executive, dying in his bath and it was obvious that Fleet Street had not been fed the whole story, or was keeping it for Monday's front pages.

Realizing that I might have to face a battery of reporters in the morning and convince them that I was nothing more than an efficient PR man, I settled down in front of a warm fire and thumbed through a number of impressive books, all on the subject of advertising.

By the time I went to bed I was pretty

confident that I could promote the sales of bi-focal lenses in East Anglia, persuade housewives in Alabama to buy black (the newest, craziest colour) or work out the percentage of porridge-eating civilians in the Greater London area. What I still didn't know, however, was exactly what Public Relations Officers were supposed to do. But this didn't stop me from sleeping some more.

* * *

Bright and early on Monday morning I got up and dressed. I studied my reflection for some time making sure that I was representative of the advertising type and couldn't help admiring the overall effect of the dark suit, white shirt, pencil slim bow tie, three-quarter white raincoat and thick horn-rimmed glasses. I reckoned I looked pretty Madison Ave. Before leaving the flat, though, I took the glasses off. They looked a bit ridiculous without lenses.

At North Park Lane House, the porter recognized me as an inmate and we smiled at each other as I waited for the aluminium lifts.

On the third floor I ambled down the mustard coloured corridor of the executives' wing to Bedlington's office and found it empty. I looked at the three telephones on the desk wondering which one I should pick up to summon his secretary, then decided that this was a golden opportunity to nose around the agency. So far, apart from the photographic studio and this room, I had only seen the Public Relations quarters housed on the ground floor.

I avoided all the rooms down the directors' corridor, not wanting to be asked awkward questions so early on, but couldn't resist a door labelled 'Media Research'.

The walls, inside this fair-sized room, were covered with charts of the British Isles which in turn were covered with little flags. Two men were reading the *Racing Gazette* while a poor thin secretary worked her fingers to the bone on some ancient typewriter. Nobody looked up, nobody cared who I was, so I decided to leave Media Research to themselves.

The other rooms on that floor seemed to have something to do with Media too and all the offices were full of people busy obviously mediaing. I found a stone staircase at the back somewhere leading down to the next floor so I took it.

The second floor was more rewarding. A pair of glass double doors had the imposing word 'CREATIVE' written blatantly across them and through the glass I could see a beehive of workers behind drawing boards, adjustable lamps, paintpots, brushes, stacks of paper and gallons of paint.

The room was long and wide and held about twenty-five artists. I walked down the centre aisle glancing at each man on either side as I went.

God, the man in charge, was at the end, a hairy individual sporting a bright green shirt with rolled up sleeves, buff suede trousers and suede boots to match.

Before I reached the halfway mark towards him, he stood up, picked up a

38

pair of thick horn-rimmed glasses, twins to the ones I had left behind, adjusted them on his pointed nose and shouted.

'What the hell do you want?'

His accent told me he had come from somewhere like the Balkans some thirty-odd years ago.

The twenty-five artists froze. One, a young man who was bravely wearing a luminous bow tie, actually smeared his layout and trembled.

'Nothing,' I said, 'I'm just looking.'

'You can't come in here and just look! Nobody comes in here to just look — nobody!!!'

From the left hand corner of the studio someone whispered a rude word. It gave me courage and I went up to the little man with hair and leaned heavily on his drawing board.

'I,' said I, 'am the new Managing Director.'

There was silence. Everyone looked up towards the little man with hair wondering what his next move would be. We were having a staring match now and I was winning. He was scared, this was his empire and without it he would be nothing at all.

'I don't remember receiving an I.O.M. about you . . . sir,' he said with certain caution.

'I don't suppose you remember receiving an I.O.M. about Harry Bedlington dying either!' I said. I hadn't the faintest idea what he was talking about, but this seemed to subdue him.

'What campaign are you working on?' I snapped.

'Chamble, Summer Campaign. Whole pages *Sunday Express*, three-inch triples *Evening Standard*.' He seemed annoyed at the thought.

'Isn't Julius working on this as well?' It was a shot in the dark.

'That Julius! He works on everything! But *I* am the creative force behind this scheme. This team, which I builded up over a number of years, is the most creative of creative teams in the whole of London!'

A rude noise came drifting across the studio from the left hand corner.

'He goes at the end of the week!'

'Who is the executive on Chamble?' I asked. I had learnt something in my books the night before. Each account or client had an executive in charge of the campaign.

'A Mr. Gear. He has as much idea about art as . . . as . . . '

'Landseer?' I suggested.

'Precisely! Precisely . . . that is exactly his attitude of mind. No imagination at all.'

I let the hairy little man get excited about this for a few minutes more before interrupting him. I knew now that I'd be able to tell him the truth without losing face.

'I'm not the new Managing Director. My name is Flute. Adam Flute. P.R. I've been called in to deal with the press over the murder.'

'Murder? Henry Bedlington was murdered?'

'Foul play hasn't been ruled out.'

Suddenly he turned and looked at every one of his artists. Like a frightened schoolroom each individual looked down at his work.

'They don't know,' he whispered to me. 'They don't know that he's even dead.'

'What about the papers?' I asked.

'These people can only read comics.'

With a neat stroke of a thick red felt pen, he added a line to the layout he was working on. Four words were already written on the sheet of cartridge paper. DON'T GAMBLE — TRY CHAMBLE. I glanced at him and he shrugged his shoulders.

'Our copywriters are very tired intellectuals.'

With the love and sympathy artists usually display towards Public Relations people, I would normally have left the studio spattered with ink and paint and possibly a slit from a razor blade down the back of my suit, but I had made friends with the studio manager now and I could leave in peace.

'Perhaps you could do something for me,' he said as he accompanied me to the door. 'Perhaps you could suggest to someone that this Mr. Gear is not quite suitable on the account.'

'Certainly,' I said, aware that I was

being sounded for some internal political conflict to come. 'Could you suggest someone to replace him?'

'Myself. I think I could handle the client far better than he does.'

I said I would see what I could do, noted that he called himself Fred Scatzikiforijikc and left the studio by the far double doors.

On my way back to Bedlington's office on the third floor, I looked in the room labelled 'COPYWRITERS'. Four of them were discussing the appalling conditions under which they had to work. They didn't realize that I was standing in the doorway and were too intent on their work to care.

Two of them were reading lurid paperbacks while the other two were engaged in an intellectual game of battleships. From a remark about Henry Bedlington I gathered that they hadn't heard about his death. There was no reason why they should have, Studio 4, where I had found his body, was the next room, but the door was closed.

Back in Bedlington's office, behind his

large half moon desk, I sat down in the comfortable hydraulic-sprung swivel chair and looked at my surroundings. Years ago an old friend of mine had ventured into the advertising jungle and before disappearing altogether had told me that anyone could make a fortune in the agency business provided they never thought too much about what they were doing. There was more confusion per square foot than in any other industry and one was paid well to complicate issues not simplify them.

As I was dwelling on how to put these thoughts into practice the door flew open and a tall blonde with deep brown eyes and an inviting mouth marched into the room.

She was twenty-five, wore grey silk trousers, a grey woollen jacket and a heavy fob bracelet. Round her neck was tied a black choker which matched her flat shoes.

'What the hell are you doing here?'

Unless she was on the board of directors I thought her a bit rude, but I swallowed my pride and didn't move.

'Please close the door behind you,' I said politely.

Put out, the blonde turned to shut the door and I had the chance of examining her from another angle. There was no doubt she was my type. Slim, long-legged, silky hair which could have been washed in any of the well advertised shampoos. I took a deep breath.

'Are you the police?' she asked coming back towards me. She was a bit frightened now and I wanted to keep it that way.

'No, I'm here to handle the press.'

'Oh. I'm sorry I was rude. I'm a little on edge.' She explained: 'I wasn't going to come in to-day but the police want to interview me. My name is Susan Trevelyan, I was Mr. Bedlington's secretary. I didn't think anyone should be in his room.'

Unexpectedly she put out her hand. A nice strong hand, with long fingernails that hadn't hit a typewriter for years.

'How do you do. A very sad affair,' I said, rising formally.

She was even taller than I had at first estimated, just an inch shorter than me, but well proportioned. I suggested she should take a seat.

'I'll be needing a secretary,' I said. 'Are you otherwise engaged?'

'No.'

She was summing me up carefully now, critically figuring out what status she would have as a second-rate typist to a third-rate PRO. The telephone rang.

'Hallo?' I said into the receiver.

'The funeral is at twelve-thirty to-morrow morning. Golders Green Crematorium. I thought I'd let you know.'

It was Ninette Bedlington being sad and cosy. I had to admit one thing about the advertising entourage, all the women were worth a second look. I thanked her for the information and assured her that I wouldn't miss the ritual for anything in the world. It would be as good a place as any for studying everybody who called themselves friends of Henry Bedlington.

I put down the receiver and met Miss Trevelyan's deep and serious gaze.

'Ninette Bedlington?' she asked.

'Yes.'

'You get around.'

'It's my job to do so.'

'She's very young.'

'But experienced.'

I let the tall blonde give me a smile and offered her a cigarette.

'Sometime,' I said, 'you must tell me who's who in this agency. Maybe we could have a session together . . . ?'

'What's wrong with my place to-night?'

Susan was an attractive piece but not irresistible. I didn't trust her any more than I did Lardvik, or Ninette, and I hadn't done anything that could make her believe I was something new on the market.

'To-night,' I said, 'I am having dinner with my mother and father.'

For a good long time she looked at me, then she got up, crossed the room seductively and opened the door. 'You have a father?'

I watched the door close on her smile and wondered whether she had closed other doors before.

I spent some time staring out of the window at the drizzle-sprayed traffic and the flaking rooftops of the double decker buses, wondering how I should go about asking more direct questions without arousing suspicion before the telephone rang.

It was Lardvik with his joint managing director's voice. He had five news reporters troubling him and he was sending them up to me. As I put down the receiver, someone banged on the door.

I adjusted my tie, pulled the swivel chair closer to the desk and wiped the grin off my face.

'Yes?' I said casually.

A redhead I hadn't seen before opened the door and showed five men in. They all wore wet coats, dripping hats and all looked around the room as though they were going to buy it.

The tallest of them came up to the desk, swept aside Henry Bedlington's favourite calendar and parked his seat in the vacant spot.

'Cigarette?'

'I'm smoking,' I said lifting my left hand to show him I wasn't lying.

'Don't remember your face.'

'Don't remember yours.'

'You're a new boy in the game, aren't you, Flute?' Another of them had come round to the side of the desk, dropped the 'out' tray on the floor and was sitting in its place.

'Not all that new, Mac,' I said. I took a corner of his coat between my fingers and felt the cloth. 'Don't they pay you well in Fleet Street any more?' We were all getting very friendly.

'Better than you'll ever get as a Private Eye, Flute,' another said from the comfort of the sofa near the television set.

'Are you working on this case privately, or helping the police?'

This, I reckoned, was all Lardvik's work. He hadn't liked the idea of me being around and nothing would get me off the premises quicker than a mention in the press.

'I'll make a deal,' I said looking at the one with the tatty coat. 'You leave me alone for a few days and I'll feed you the whole story when I've got it, for nothing.'

That was all they wanted. They grinned

at each other and all looked at the tall one.

'Got a lead we can hand the Editor to keep *him* happy?'

'Yes,' I said, flicking my cigarette ash towards the ashtray, but missing. 'It's believed that the formula of the new Chamble powder, which formed the basis of Bedlington's death bath, contained a high percentage of caustic soda.'

They knew it wasn't true, but it was a good story. That's all the news boys expected of a good Public Relations man, a good story. The public would swallow it — they always did.

4

Golders Green Crematorium on a wet November morning isn't the best place to chew cheese and chutney sandwiches, but that's exactly what I was doing as I sat in my car parked just inside the gates with Susan Trevelyan sitting right next to me eating a banana.

She had called unexpectedly at the flat round about eleven to cadge a lift to the crematorium, and the fact that she had cooked me up a cup of coffee while I got dressed did in a way endear her to me. Besides she had a certain amount of common sense, like suggesting I should wear a black suit for the occasion and not green tweed.

Now we sat and listened to 'music-while-you-work' played on a terrible theatre organ and I wondered whether the stoker in the boiler house behind the chapel was tuned in to the same programme.

Susan suddenly nudged me fiercely with her elbow and I looked up to see a long light blue Rolls Royce coming through the gates. The car matched the driver's eyes.

Julius Lardvik got out and walked round the huge machine to open the door for his passenger. The girl who appeared caused a mild tremor to run through Susan's body. She looked like a warm ripe fruit from the Mediterranean. Dark with shiny black hair, she had almond-shaped eyes with deep brown irises and a full mouth, high cheek bones like a Slav statue and a head which stood majestically on a swan-like neck. I fancied her.

'Who's that?' I asked, taking my hand off Susan's knee to remove a piece of chutney from between my front teeth.

'Clementine Deshalles.'

'And what is she to the agency?'

'A bitch!'

I watched Julius take Clementine's arm and lead her slowly into the mausoleum where we were all soon to pay our last tributes to the man who had died unconventionally.

From the way she walked I figured Clementine was no ordinary member of the staff, but a side glance at Susan warned me to lay off the subject for a while.

After Lardvik's car quite a number of others poured in, all shapes and sizes. Some chauffeur driven, some young executive driven, some driven beautifully by women, others driven aggressively by frustrated old men. It seemed the advertising industry had turned out in full to see this 'great' man go.

'They don't usually die so young in this field of the rat race,' Susan said wiping a solitary tear from her left eye. 'They have ulcers and get the sack or go broke, but they don't usually die.' It was obvious that Henry Bedlington had gone up in her esteem since he had departed.

After some fifty cars had backed, gone forward, reversed again and turned to get themselves in the parking lot, a large crimson van appeared and stopped outside the gates. Written across the side panels, in lime green, was the endearing word 'Chamble'. Some tactful genius had probably gone to some lengths to think up this little throw away bouquet.

Two young men in jeans leapt out of the van, flung open the back doors and pulled out a very long spray of flowers. They laid it down near the chapel steps for everyone to see and Susan explained that it was a parting gift from the staff. I thought it a pity that the flowers were artificial, but they were going to be used in a photographic session later in the week.

The hearse, which had made an unhazardous journey from the morgue near Scotland Yard, finally drew up in the area and four lurid men got out, fitted themselves with black top hats and rolled out the jolly coffin.

The wreaths, many of them, were carefully taken down from the roof of the hearse and carried ceremoniously to the red brick suburban cloister, the walls of which were crammed with little notices about who was sleeping there.

With interest I watched a number of elderly people clamber out of the funeral cars which followed the hearse, and sat up when I noticed the slim, small, fascinating figure of Ninette. She was holding onto some aged man's arm, her father-in-law, and was still having trouble convincing people she was sad.

As I attempted to get out of the car to follow the procession of people into the chapel, I was nearly knocked down by a Mini Minor which came to a halt half an inch from the crematorium wall.

A small neat man got out energetically, slammed the door noisily and turned round to beam at Susan.

'Hi, Suzy! Free for dinner to-night?'

'Everard! What are you doing here?' She was beginning to giggle. It seemed that this man was going to be the comic turn of the morning.

Everard blinked. He apparently blinked whenever he was excited and as he was excited all the time he never stopped blinking. Round his neck hung two cameras and a light meter, which seemed to have been there since he was born.

'Pay my last respects — take a picture or two. Can one see the flames from the pews?'

He smiled a quick nervous smile and glanced at me. He seemed to think I was going to shoot him or something.

'This is Everard Philbear,' Susan said. 'The reasonably famous photographer.'

I put out my hand and blinked to keep him company.

He was really very highly strung.

'You're Adam Flute, aren't you? The private detective. I remember taking your photograph during that model murder affair — I was on the *Daily Mail* then.'

I tightened my grip on his hand and made him wince. He blinked a few times more before getting the message, then tried to make up for it by whispering, in a perfectly audible voice, something about no one having heard.

As Susan was standing right next to me, she heard everything and stood back to look at me. She was surprised, admirative and concerned. She flashed on her nervous smile and looked at me some more. She liked exciting men.

A thundering organ note from within the chapel called us to worship, and we walked up the entrance steps and into the

damp gloom of the departures platform
— Golders Green.

* * *

It was just as the priest had said the last
few words of the ritual and sent the coffin
flying down the rails through the little
curtains and into the fiery furnace that
Everard Philbear nudged me and, grin-
ning from ear to ear, handed me two
photographs.

Technically they were beautiful. Full
colour shots of a lovely young nude in
quite moral positions. She had dark
bobbed hair and a most attractive silky
dark skin with pleasant little breasts. I
thought it was very nice to know that
Ninette was even better without clothes
on.

'How much?' I asked, slipping the
photographs into my wallet.

'Not mine to sell I'm afraid. I didn't
take them.'

'Who did?'

Ninette Bedlington, fully dressed in a
black suit and wearing a Persian lamb

coat, was at that very moment coming down the aisle on her father-in-law's arm. Behind her was Lardvik keeping close to the Mediterranean fruit.

'Who do you think? Blue-eyed blondy there, the one with the beard.'

*   *   *

Since Everard Philbear already knew who I was and seemed to know more about the private lives of the agency staff than anyone else I had met, I accepted his invitation to a drink which he offered as we left the crematorium.

After dropping Susan off at the agency and making her promise to keep her mouth shut about my real identity, I managed to find a parking place in Mayfair and walked the remaining half mile to his studios, in a mews off Curzon Street.

The receptionist was coloured. That is to say she had pink hair, green eye shadow and white lips to match her face. As soon as I came in she stood up and pretended to recognize me.

'Mr. Flute, Mr. Philbear will see you right away.'

I walked up a narrow flight of steps at the top of which I found myself on a balcony overlooking a vast barn-like studio full of complicated electrical fittings, hanging gardens, acres of white paper and various papier mâché props. Sitting at a refectory table in the middle of it all was Everard, now sporting a heavy knit fisherman's sweater, jeans and a beret.

Finding my way down another narrow flight of steps I sat down opposite him at the table and looked at the fashionable photographer who had stopped blinking because he was deep in thought.

'I think I ought to come clean,' he said, suddenly looking up, then looking down at his fingernails. 'I think I was the last person to see Bedlington alive.'

I said nothing but watched him work out his next sentence carefully.

'I was taking the Chamble photographs in the agency studios with him on the afternoon of the murder. We had been having a fair amount of trouble getting the bath to bubble and had emptied six bottles of soda water into it before achieving the right result, by which time the model who was supposed to be in it had gone off to powder her nose.' He was cleaning his nails with the corner of a negative now. 'I went to call her, and when I got back, the door was closed.'

I still said nothing. Somewhere I had learnt never to interrupt people when they are in a confessing mood.

'As Bedlington was a very busy man and apt to change his mind about things anyway, I didn't think much about it and went home. It was only when I read the report of his death in the papers the following day that I realized I was the last to see him.'

'Who was in the agency when you left?' I asked.

'The usual army of idiots who kid everyone they are hard workers by staying after hours.'

'Any suspects?'

At this moment tea was brought in by Everard's Technicolor receptionist. He had invited me for a drink, but then hadn't specified what type. The girl put down a tray of Etruscan tea cups and looked at her employer.

'You will be careful of those mugs, won't you? We're photographing them for the British Museum.'

The tea, I guessed, had also come from the British Museum when I took my first sip, but being stoic, and hungry, I leaned more heavily on my elbows and stared at Everard without complaining.

'Who do you suspect?' I asked, repeating my question.

'Frankly, I don't know. Lardvik has a motive.'

There was no doubt that people were gunning for the tall blonde adman from Scandinavia. Ninette had hinted he might be worth suspecting, and now Everard was naming him. But somewhere something didn't seem right. I wasn't sure why I had been handed the photographs, and I certainly didn't like the idea of Ninette being on nude-photographic terms with Lardvik.

As I looked up I saw Everard glancing quickly away. For some time now he had been studying me. I trusted him and his stories as much as everyone else.

'Who hired you?' he asked after a while.

'I never disclose the names of my clients,' I said professionally.

'No, of course not. I shouldn't have asked.'

'I'm not working on the murder anyway. I'm trying to find out who's been supplying certain information to another agency.'

He was only mildly interested, which surprised me, so I told him a bit more.

'A firm called Cordite Advertising Ltd. came out with an advertisement which was exactly the same as one Lardvik had designed for Chamble last month, and have announced a Spring Campaign for Chamble's rival — 'Barfnite' — which is identical to another of Lardvik's ideas.'

'Really?' Everard was being polite, he was bored with anything to do with agencies and couldn't raise any enthusiasm for the bit of gossip I had handed him. But I went on trying.

'Do you know anyone at Cordite Advertising?'

If he did, he never had the chance to tell me, because the receptionist bird came in again, this time wearing a false smile.

'The model's here for the Sitwell Girdle ad,' she said.

'Ah! Yes, well, could you tell her to come right in. Mr. Flute, you'll have to excuse me, unless you'd like to stay and watch. The girl's not very attractive but the girdle is not bad at all.'

He shone a dazzling smile and blinked in my direction and I realized it was time to go.

As I left the studio, climbing up the narrow stairs to the balcony, I met the Girdle Girl. She had nothing on except a thick woollen dress, two sweaters and a mohair coat. Her face was wrapped in a shawl to prevent the cold wind ruining that valuable complexion, and though I felt there was something worth seeing underneath all the disguise, I didn't allow myself the spare time to stay. As I left, she was shivering and looking at the

63

cold cement floor.

'We'll have the first one of you lying down here, when you're ready, Miss Humbert.'

I nodded to Miss Technicolor on the way out and did up the top button of my overcoat as I hit the icy north wind which was on its way through the mews.

I managed to get my car before the attendant could stick his yellow label on it, and shrugged my shoulders as he checked his watch with the parking meter. I had enough puzzles to work out and wouldn't have worried about an extra ten bob fine right then. What I did care about was whether little Ninette was having an affair with her godfather, and if so why she was throwing me onto his scent. Why, come to think of it, had she called me at all?

When I reached the third floor of North Park Lane House and Bedlington's comfortable office, the answer wasn't made any simpler.

Standing in the middle of the bright orange carpet, with his feet well apart, his bloated chest locked inside a thick black-dyed army coat and a bowler impelled on his turnip-like shape, was my old friend Detective Inspector Bowels. He was the sort of man anyone would fall in love with, his main attraction being his eyelashless eyes and thin black moustache.

Looking out of the window, within easy reach of the big man, was my other friend, Detective Sergeant Frank Chaucer. They made a lovely pair, both of them, with not a chromosome of humour between them.

'Good afternoon, gentlemen,' I said, smiling to annoy them. 'I hope I haven't kept you waiting — or was it someone else you came to see?'

'Ever seen this before?' Bowels asked without ceremony.

Between his kid-gloved fingertips he was holding a small polythene bag with 'CHAMBLE' printed on it.

'I'm not sure,' I said, not sure.

'You must have done, Mr. Flute. We found it in your white raincoat pocket, hanging right here behind the door.'

I was surprised. I didn't remember ever

picking up a polythene bag and putting it in my raincoat pocket. Come to think of it I didn't remember leaving my raincoat hanging behind the door.

'The trouble is, Flute, that there is only one of these bags in the world, you see. This is a prototype. The word 'Chamble' here and the slogan 'A laugh with every bath' here, have only been painted on, and, unfortunately, this bag is believed to be the murder weapon, the one used to suffocate Mr. Bedlington. Have you anything to say?'

At that moment Chaucer turned to face me and actually smiled. It was this that made me go pale and prompted the original phrase from Bowels: 'You don't look too well, Flute. Perhaps you had better come with us to talk over your problem.'

5

It was the first time I had been invited to an early tea at Savile Row police station and I found the place as colourful as any British Railways waiting room.

Bowels removed his bowler, handing it to Chaucer, fingered his moustache and stroked his lantern jaw. He knew I wasn't guilty of the murder of Henry Bedlington but he suspected me of knowing a lot more about the crime than I did.

He suggested I should sit down on a hard-backed chair opposite him, so I did.

'Well,' he began, with a heavy sigh, 'how did this polythene bag get into your pocket?'

'I suppose someone put it there.'

'Is there any reason why anyone should?'

'Not that I can think of.'

'Why were you at the funeral this morning?'

'I work for the agency, a matter of decency.'

'Why do you work at the agency?'

'I have to earn a living like you, Mr. Bowels. You must know that business hasn't been too good lately.'

This remark produced a twitch on the left side of his mouth which I suspected might be a smile. It stopped the immediate barrage of questions anyway.

'Acting as a Public Relations Officer may excuse you for being mixed up in this business, but it doesn't explain why this polythene bag, which we consider to be exhibit number one, was found in your raincoat pocket.'

Anyone could have planted the bag, and that was obviously what had happened, but I would have difficulty in convincing friend Bowels. There was no doubt, however, that whoever had originally tried to incriminate me hadn't yet given up.

'When I joined the agency I bought myself a new trousseau,' I said with a bored voice and an innocent expression. 'Being an adman I had to have a white

68

raincoat. The first day I hung it up, on the hooks provided in the gentlemen's cloakroom, and in the evening when I was ready to leave there were thirty-four others like it. I suggest that either I picked up the wrong one, or whoever wanted to plant the bag, planted it in the wrong coat. There are a number of other possible explanations.'

Bowels was interested. The idea of a mistake appealed to him and he glanced at Chaucer who glanced back. They might be onto something important. Bowels stood up suddenly, forcing me to do likewise.

'I'm letting you go this time, Flute, but if I find that you're more mixed up in this than you pretend, I swear I won't give you a second chance.'

Outside, in the dreary drizzle of Savile Row, I hailed a taxi and went straight back to the agency. Someone was trying to land me with a murder rap, and I was going to find out who that someone was, even if it meant a long, slow, boring process of elimination.

Back in Bedlington's office, now cold

and dark with most of the other offices empty, I sat down at the desk and looked down the list of the staff that Susan had managed to get me.

There were plenty of names, three hundred and four in all, but none of them told me anything.

I played around with the hydraulic swivel chair for a while and even toyed with the idea of watching television, when I recalled the funeral and the people I had seen there. One person, I felt sure, would know plenty about the Bedlington-Lardvik set-up, and that was the Clementine girl.

I thumbed through the staff list again looking for someone who might give me a lead to her, then realized it was probably too late and everyone would have gone home, but Everard had talked about the 'idiots' who stayed at the office late, so I took myself for a walk.

There was no one on the third, or second floor, but on the first I saw a light and stopped in front of the door which bore the name F. GEAR.

In a comfortable little room with a

large window overlooking the black night of the park lit up by the stream of homegoing cars, sat Mr. Gear, talking on the telephone.

He was about twenty-eight, had short curly hair, attractive features, a good smile, intense blue eyes and a frown which told everybody that though young he was serious and dedicated.

He suggested by a wave of an executive hand that I should sit down and offered me a cigarette.

After telling someone at the other end of the line to hurry up with the blocks and to make sure that they had the right insertion, he put down the receiver and turned his full charming attention on me.

After a brief introduction, a mild shake of the hand, I asked him to put me in the picture *vis à vis* Chamble. As far as he was concerned I was the new PR on the job, nothing more.

He talked non-stop for twenty minutes without telling me anything I wanted to know before I could ask him a few pertinent questions on the agency and its staff.

Starting with Lardvik, he told me that he thought him an overrated creative man, but clever with figures. He and Bedlington had never seen eye to eye and it was a mystery to everyone why they had ever become associated. He knew nothing of his private life which didn't concern anyone anyway.

About Fred Scatzikiforijikc he said little. He was known as Fred Scatz and was impossible to work with. A brilliant artist who spent his whole time telling other people how to do their own jobs without getting on with his own.

When I asked about Susan Trevelyan, a genuine smile crossed his face. It seemed that she was the agency's pride and joy. She had a beautiful flat overlooking the Thames near Hammersmith Bridge and nearly everyone of importance in the agency had at one time been allowed to admire the view. If I really wanted to know about the intrigues of the firm I couldn't pick anyone better — besides if I had a car and a fair amount of loot, nothing could be simpler than arranging a tête-à-tête.

Henry Bedlington, as far as he was concerned, had been very much the boss, far more so than Julius Lardvik who had no idea how to handle people. Lardvik was apt to moan and dawdle, to criticize his fellow directors rather than get on with the work. But Gear had only been in this particular agency for two years and didn't know too much about the management's background.

He had only seen Ninette Bedlington once, in her husband's car. He had never met her personally and only knew that she was very beautiful if a little small.

About Francis Gear himself I gathered that he had been in advertising eight years, that he was contemplating marriage early next year, but that at the moment he could think of nothing else but the promotion of Chamble. I felt a little sorry for him, but he was happy enough.

Without arousing his suspicion I steered the name of Clementine Deshalles into the conversation and eventually got the information I wanted. She was not on the permanent staff, but an out-of-work actress who had recently made a success of her life by appearing in TV advertisements as the 'Chamble Girl'. She lived in a flat in South Kensington, and any time I wanted to contact her to arrange publicity all I had to do was call. She was publicity mad, and didn't mind men. Very kindly, all part of the work to promote the soap bubbles, he wrote down her address on a piece of paper, and I left his office.

* * *

I parked the car in Drayton Gardens and walked down the road to the block of flats where Clementine lived. It was one of those Victorian affairs which don't look too oppressive, with a couple of inches of garden between the street and the main entrance.

I took the lift up to the second floor and rang the bell. As I did so I noticed the door was in actual fact open, so I pushed it gently and stepped into the apartment.

It was a fair-sized flat furnished in a feminine way. The living room curtains were drawn but I managed to find a standard lamp and switched it on. Either she was a very untidy girl or there had been a struggle. The long sofa in front of the fireplace was upside down, all the drawers of a chest in one corner had been pulled out and the contents strewn all over the floor, a hundred or so books had been pulled out of the book case and hurled across the room, and the glass of an antique cabinet had been smashed.

Fearing the worst I rushed into the next room and found it in a similar condition. The large double mattress had been pulled off the base, the cupboards had been wrenched open and all her dresses strewn over the floor, a long arm had swept an arc over her dressing table and all her make-up lay broken and oozing on the pink carpet.

In the kitchen the ransackers hadn't had such a good time. The larder hadn't been highly stocked but they had managed to smear the walls with butter.

I walked quickly back to the living room and hunted around for some sort of clue, an object maybe which might give me some idea why all this had happened, and in one of the pulled out drawers I found something which could have been significant.

It was a photograph of the Worthing Repertory Company taken on the pier. Among the disillusioned actors and actresses I could only recognize two faces. One was Clementine Deshalles', the other was Ninette.

Deciding that my best bet was to leave the flat and wait outside to see what happened, I switched off the standard lamp and closed the living room door. As I was about to start down the stairs, I remembered one room I hadn't been in.

With my heart in my mouth I went back and tried the handle on the bathroom door. It answered. Slowly I pushed, went into the small tiled room, switched on the bright light and stared down into the bath.

It was empty, but for a piece of foolscap paper. On it someone had typed a message, it read:

Careless talk costs lives — maybe yours.

6

Careless talk costs lives. It wasn't a very original slogan but then advertising personnel had the habit of cribbing. I looked at the note as intelligently as I could without having the faintest idea who might have written it, then dropped it, watching the piece of paper float clumsily down into the bath.

Clementine was going to be in need of protection if it wasn't already too late. Ninette, come to that, might also be in danger. I decided to pay my client a visit to talk over the sequence of events again.

★   ★   ★

I rang the doorbell a couple of times before the door was opened. I wasn't sure whether Ninette employed a maid or not but I didn't expect to see Chaucer opening up for me.

He was pleased that I had come, but

not Bowels who was, for some unaccountable reason, sitting on the stairs.

'I'm sorry to bother you,' I said as pleasantly as I could, 'but I left some important papers with Mrs. Bedlington which I need at the office to-morrow.'

Bowels rose slowly to his feet, sighed a deep sigh and glanced sideways at Chaucer.

'You're beginning to bore me, Flute. However I would be interested to know where she's been taken to and why?'

I didn't say anything for quite a time because I was thinking. The door of the drawing room was open and I could see a certain amount of disorder. The lamp-stand for one thing had been knocked over and one of the paintings was hanging crookedly on the wall. Had she been paid a visit too?

'Ninette Bedlington, you mean?' I said inquisitively just to make sure I had surmised rightly.

'Ninette Bedlington,' he said dimpling his cheeks.

'I didn't know,' I said frankly, 'that she wouldn't be here.'

'No?'

'No.'

'Well you know now. Any intrepid ideas? We were rung by an anonymous caller telling us that Mrs. Bedlington had been abducted. It was a woman caller.'

'With a soft voice?'

'Yes. You know her?'

'No.'

'Why did you ask?'

'Some women have hard voices.'

They allowed me to go into the drawing room. The orange curtains were drawn back and I was pleased to see that the French windows opened onto a terrace. Chaucer was standing a few feet behind me which didn't help me to get any brilliant ideas. There was no doubt that I was worried; to lose one's client so early in an investigation wasn't very good for the record. I would have to do something terribly clever.

I looked around the room again and stared at the desk. After getting Chaucer's permission to do so I opened the drawer and brought out the address book which Ninette had shown me. I thumbed through it expertly and turned to my name. I gasped, breathed out a whistle and turned to Chaucer.

'Your boss seen this?' I exclaimed, putting on the big frown.

'What?'

'My name, here, in Bedlington's book. Significant, don't you think?'

I liked Chaucer because he took his job so seriously. He was amazed at being handed a piece of evidence by me and, without pausing to realize that it meant nothing, snatched the book from my hands and rushed out of the room to give it to Bowels.

With as much energy I rushed to the french windows, threw them open and leapt out into the drizzling night, nearly twisting an ankle and fracturing my skull by falling down two unexpected steps. But I managed to hide in the shadows of some bushes before the detectives realized what had happened.

The drizzle, for once, was in my favour. Even the two policemen who were supposed to be circumnavigating the house for clues helped by panicking. They were smoking behind the garage when Bowels blew his whistle, and this sent them running in every direction but mine. Their torches proved useless in the fine spray and while they argued I gently moved through the undergrowth till I reached an open space. Across a long, smooth, safe lawn, there was a wall with a wrought-iron gate opening onto a street lit by an old gas lamp.

Taking a deep breath I ran across the lawn and reached the gate. A glance over my shoulder told me that Bowels was still dithering around the terrace trying to see in the dark.

A brisk walk down the civilized streets of Primrose Hill eventually led me to the main Regent's Park road and a bus stop. I waited a minute or two, hopped on the first that came along and got off at the first set of traffic lights. A few seconds later a taxi drew up to my hand wave and I got in.

I hadn't a moment to lose and I told the driver that it was more than a matter of life and death, it was a matter of him getting five pounds if he could get me to

Hammersmith in ten minutes. With Ninette missing and Clementine in danger I had visions of the one person who had helped me quite a lot meeting an unpleasant end. Susan was just as involved as anyone else in the Bedlington case and it was my duty to save her. There was also the possibility that she might help me some more.

As we raced through the heavy traffic, some people were still hoping to get to their dress circle seats in time for the second act; the thought occurred to me that I might be up against a gang and not an individual. It was a heroic idea considering I was heading straight for a possible danger area.

The taxi got me there in twenty-five minutes which wasn't bad going. I gave him the best part of ten shillings for his efforts and didn't wait to be thanked.

A thick white mist was lurking over the Thames and the silence for London was eerie. Any second I expected to see the ghost of a hansom cab coming over Hammersmith Bridge, but all I saw was the beautiful metallic smoothness of

Lardvik's blue Rolls parked, quite neatly, outside a tall ugly block of flats.

The place was no luxury affair with stone stairs leading to all floors. I started the trying climb, thinking that it wasn't representative of Susan's personality, then remembering that she had probably inherited the flat from her parents who might have had to work harder for their living than she had. Her name was engraved on a small copper plate outside the last door on the top floor.

I rang the bell, hammered the knocker and waited patiently. The door was part wood and part glass and painted green; like all Council Flats the stairway smelt of disinfectant. Eventually the door opened.

Her long smooth silky golden hair hung down to her shoulders and her pale pink lips caressed the thin black end of a long cigarette holder. She was wearing black and scarlet cossack pyjamas with toreador style pants, a few fluid ounces of frenzy-making scent and no bra.

'Were you going to bed?' I asked.

'Not immediately.'

'May I come in?'

She wasn't hurrying her invitation. She was smiling plenty and giving me encouraging enough looks, but she was waiting for the other visitor to clear out. I tried to look beyond her but there was only a wall with a closed door in it. I sniffed once or twice and looked entranced.

'Nice smell,' I said.

'Double Entente by Pajacou.'

'A pleasant Havana tang about it,' I said, smiling at her eyes.

'Oh that! I've been smoking cigarlettes.'

I was still outside the front door and it was getting draughty.

'Can't I come in now — he must have gone.'

'Who?'

'Julius. His car is a little obvious, you know. Or would you like me to come another day?'

'No. No, come in — but wait here.'

I came in and waited there, just inside the front door in a small cubicle of a hall with a Russell-Flint reproduction hanging on one wall and a light switch stuck in the middle of another.

Behind the door Susan had gone through I heard a bit of shuffling. I didn't even bother to bend down and have a look at the keyhole, I could sense what was going on. Where's my hat, my coat, he mustn't see me here . . . you can always say it was my chauffeur or a friend I lend the car to. I smiled, just as the door opened.

'You were wrong, of course, darling,' she said taking my left lapel in her right hand in way of suggesting I should take my coat off. 'It wasn't Julius. A friend of his borrows his car.'

My overcoat came off easily and we stood there together studying the intricate weave of the tweed material. Then I moved a little towards her. I hadn't said anything about my passion for blondes dressed in black and scarlet cossack pyjamas, but she seemed to guess how I felt. As she moved her hand up my back inside my jacket, I moved mine behind her back inside her cossack pyjamas. She was at the disadvantage, I was wearing a waistcoat, drip-dry shirt and double-knit combed-cotton underwear.

After seven minutes of emotional splendour and three minutes of cramp in my right arm, she released me and just kept hold of my hand.

'A drink?'

'Please.' I was regaining my breath and adjusting my tie.

The flat was small but well furnished with thick carpets, contemporary furniture and this panoramic view of the river. When the lights were out I guessed one could see the watery night life of London going on down below, if one was allowed to look in that direction.

Susan handed me a Rye and Dry and sat me down on a long peacock-blue rubber-sprung job which pretended to be a sofa for decency's sake. In front of me was a wide angled television set, to the left a Hi-Fi record player and behind me by a door that led to the rest of the flat a rather flashy cocktail cabinet. On the top of a dresser there was a framed photograph of a pretty little girl with a sarcastic smile. It didn't mean anything to me but a sudden rush of air in the room behind me and the sound of the front door closing did. Lardvik had left.

'Are we alone now?' I asked.

'We always were, darling.'

She was fitting one of those black cigarettes into her holder and putting on a big act for my benefit. I watched her pick up her glass from the mantelpiece and drop down to kneel at my feet on the high white pile of the carpet. She was a cosy creature.

'I'm not staying,' I said in case she had any ideas about prolonging the evening.

'Why did you come then?'

'Ask you a few questions.'

'Are you working to-night then?'

'I'm always working.'

She looked at me over the rim of her glass. Her eyes had that innocent look which needed confirmation.

'What do you want to know?'

For a moment I felt I had heard her voice before, the deep soft tone of it, warm and sensual.

'I want to know how well Ninette Bedlington knew Clementine.'

'Why ask me, I . . . what do you mean knew?'

'I visited Clementine's flat to-night — it's been ransacked. I also visited Ninette's house, and she's missing.'

Her mouth opened attractively to signify that she was surprised by the news. What surprised me was that her eyes kept darting from my face to the door behind me.

'Because Mrs. Bedlington's missing, it doesn't mean that anything has happened though, does it?'

'That's what I want to find out. I thought you might help.'

She wasn't looking at me at all now, so I started to turn to see what was going on that was so interesting. It was a shadow, a big one, bulky, black, holding an ugly sap in one of its hands. The sap hit me across the left temple and I keeled over to fall in a heap on the white pile with my Rye and Dry fizzing under me.

The sounds of their voices were dim, but I could tell by the tone of Susan's voice that she was surprised. She was kind enough to repeat a sentence a few times anyway, which I knew would help me when I woke up.

'You shouldn't have, Julius,' she kept on saying. 'You shouldn't have.' I smiled bravely and let go.

7

I woke up between a pair of blue silk sheets in her bed. I had nothing on except my gold wrist watch and a pair of black socks; the curtains were still drawn but badly enough to leave enough light through to let me know where I was.

It was just on seven o'clock and the side of my head throbbed to remind me what had happened. I sat up, shivered, looked around for my clothes and decided to slip down again into the warmth of the womb-like bed.

On the bedside table there was a glass of water and a tube of aspirins, also a piece of paper with something scribbled on it. I grabbed hold of the aspirins, helped myself to a threesome, swallowed them with the help of the icy water and held up the piece of paper to read the message.

The note was folded in four, and when I unfolded it I found myself holding a piece of foolscap with a short typewritten sentence. The curtains didn't allow enough light to read by, so I got out of bed and went to the window.

The view was pretty good, of Hammersmith Bridge and a couple of barges steaming along underneath, but the piece of foolscap was more interesting. It was the same one that I had seen in Clementine's flat, with the added scribble on the top fold.

The scribble was in a childish handwriting but it told me who it was from.

Sorry about what happened. Will explain. Will also look after you. Please call when you wake up.

Love, Susan.

The door opened as I finished reading the message, but quickly closed again. Gallantly I got back into bed and shouted that all was clear.

Susan, wrapped in the warmth of a thin silk dressing-gown, came in carrying a couple of cups of black coffee. She was all made up and looking remarkably attractive for that time of the morning.

'I heard you moving about, thought you'd like this.'

'I wouldn't mind my clothes.'

'They're in the next room.'

She sat down on the edge of the bed and handed me my cup. I was in no mood to kiss her good morning but felt well enough to wish that I was.

'It hurts to talk right now,' I said. 'So you just tell me what happened.'

'I promised I wouldn't.'

She was lighting two cigarettes and one of them was for me. I took it between my lips and inhaled. I was recovering rapidly.

'Who did you promise you wouldn't?'

'The person who hit you.'

'What did you promise? That you wouldn't tell me what happened or that you wouldn't tell me who he was?'

'Nothing happened. It was just a mistake. I have jealous friends.'

I hadn't been badly treated by her, and she was being pretty nice. In her innocence she might have seen it as a jealous attack, but I was puzzled by the note.

'This note you wrote me, where did you get the paper from?'

'Why?'

'I'm just interested. It has something written on the other side.'

'The man . . . who hit you gave it to me . . . He had it in his pocket.'

I wondered how many others he had like it. Was he doing the rounds delivering them to all his girl friends? I realized now that I had surprised the supposed stranger and probably saved Susan a fair amount of trouble — if not her life.

'Who was it?' I asked looking deeply into her eyes.

'I promised I wouldn't tell you.'

'Look, Suzy, you're a nice girl, young, beautiful, a good future in front of you . . . I don't want you to get hurt. That man is dangerous.' I was beginning to get an American accent.

'I promised.'

I gripped both her arms and twisted her so that she had to look at me. Her thin silk dressing-gown slid open in the front and I looked at the beautiful little gold and enamel St. Christopher which hung from her neck.

'Who was it?' My grip had tightened noticeably and she looked at me just a tiny bit frightened.

'I'm not going to tell you, but you know perfectly well who it was.'

I let go of her and sank back against the ample pillows. So it had been Lardvik and he had found it necessary to knock me out to hide his presence. His secrets were obviously well worth investigating.

'Can I have my clothes?'

'Of course.'

'Well, I'm going to clear out of here and go back to my flat, and go through the day as though nothing had happened. And I want you to do the same.'

She was standing up now, a little frightened maybe by my severe tone of voice.

'He didn't mean to hit you so hard. He just has a terrible temper. I thought he'd gone.'

She left the room only to come back a few seconds later with my shirt and trousers.

'Would you like a hot bath? It would

help you relax a little.'

'Do I need relaxing?'

'You look pretty excited about something!'

She was sitting on the edge of the bed again and feeling the side of my face with her cool finger tips. Just for something to do I reached out for her medallion. I wanted to have a closer look, being a lover of beautiful things.

★   ★   ★

The morning papers told me that Ninette Bedlington, whose husband's body had been found immersed in a bath of dangerous acid by intrepid Scotland Yard Chief Frank Chaucer, was missing, believed dead.

I didn't believe she was dead and poured a bit more dangerous acid powder into my bath watching it froth up rather unsensationally. It was only the thought of using the little packet of Chamble, which Susan had said I would find in the bathroom cupboard, that had given me the incentive to get up at all.

Hidden two inches under the Chamble foam I waited patiently for the carbon dioxide bubbles to appear so that my skin would be cleansed and bleached like never before. No bubbles appeared, even when I agitated, and when I let myself slide down further in the bath I realized the foam had one great disadvantage, it got into my nose.

I was thinking how I could best find out where Ninette had got to when the thought occurred to me that the whole of the London police force was probably out looking for me. I had, after all, given Bowels the slip the night before. If I didn't act soon I would find myself trapped by Mr. Bowels's boring efficiency.

I stayed in the bath a few seconds longer, then pulled out the plug. Very slowly the level coating of shining white foam fell like the scum on the Thames at Boulter's Lock and my two shining white knees appeared. They were cold, so I got out.

After a very good cup of coffee in the small tidy kitchen which sported a red refrigerator, Susan fed me a couple of fried eggs, toast and marmalade. She had drawn her blonde hair back in a bun and looked attractively severe as any good secretary should.

'Are you going to the agency this morning?' she asked.

'I expect so.'

'Shall I come with you, or don't you think we'd better be seen together?'

'If Lardvik is looking out for you, I think it would be very unwise. You go ahead — I'll drop into my flat on the way and change my suit.'

'You might see a doctor about that bruise, it doesn't look very happy.'

'It'll be all right. Could I use your telephone?'

She said I could and I took my coffee into the living room and settled down on the peacock-blue settee with the instrument on my lap. I dialled Scotland Yard and asked for Bowels. He was in, but tired.

'Where did you get to?' I asked, as though I cared.

'I'm going to pull you in, Flute. You

were escaping arrest!'

'Escaping arrest? What were you arresting me for?'

'You're a suspect.'

'Well, I wasn't escaping.'

'No? What were you doing?'

'I was running after that man!'

'What man?'

'The man who was in the garden. I just saw him on the terrace. I shouted for you, but you wouldn't help.'

'Did you see him?'

'Vaguely — but he got away. There was a gate at the bottom of the garden giving onto a street.'

'Yes, that's right. It was open when we got there. What did he look like?'

I dried up for a moment, I hadn't thought of that question. I couldn't say it was Lardvik, that would have been a direct accusation. I stalled till someone came to mind.

'He was small, wore glasses I think. Suede shoes and yes . . . suede trousers, also a green shirt.'

'That Bulgarian artist fellow!'

Bowels rang off quite suddenly and I

put down my own receiver. I felt a little freer, less hunted anyway; while they were chasing him, I'd have time to do a bit more investigating.

'You know there's the Chamble Creative Presentation meeting this afternoon,' Susan said coming in to pick up her fur coat.

'The what?'

'Creative Presentation — Chamble. This is the big day when the agency shows the client how they intend spending his money in the next year. They'll be showing some of the advertisements all the fuss is about.'

'I'd better be there then?'

'If that's really what you're after.'

I didn't like her quite so much with her hair back, she looked prim and unapproachable.

'What time does it start?'

'Two o'clock sharp.'

'I'll be there.'

She gave me a brief kiss on the forehead, as though we'd been married for years, and left the flat. I took my coffee cup back to the kitchen, left it on the draining board and followed her a few minutes later. Since waking up that morning I had intended paying Clementine's apartment another visit. I was still going to keep the appointment, though three hours late on schedule.

I half expected the police to be surrounding the block of flats so I stopped the taxi at the end of the road and walked the rest of the way. But no police were around.

On the second floor the coast was clear and a couple of milk bottles were even neatly standing outside her door to show that nothing had happened. Surprised, curious, I rang the bell.

A few moments later the door opened and I found myself looking at Clementine herself. She was dressed in a slim donkey-grey suit and looked calm and more beautiful than I remembered her.

'Yes?' she asked.

She had an attractive smile and lovely teeth, her eyes were a deep black, large, almond shaped, her skin, possibly a little sallow, gave her that exciting Oriental aura.

'Yes?' she said again, a little impatiently.

'Are you all right?' I asked.

'Shouldn't I be?'

'You had some trouble last night.'

'Who are you to tell me?'

'I can hardly explain out here.'

Reluctantly she opened her door wider and I stepped into the familiar apartment. Unlike the night before it was clean, tidy and pleasantly homely.

'My name is Adam Flute. I'm a Private Investigator.'

'Oh?'

'I'm working for Bedlington, Lardvik Advertising Ltd., on a case of creative leakages. I happened to drop by last night to see you.'

'What about?'

'A few questions concerning agency staff.'

'I know very few of them.'

'Ninette Bedlington?'

'A little. She's not part of the agency though.'

'Did you know that she was missing?'

'No.'

She didn't want to show her surprise at

the news nor the fact that it frightened her, but I saw her tighten her grip on the door-knob as we went into the living-room.

'You did know that your flat had been broken into last night though.'

'My brother and his friends had a party. He is a teenager and a little reckless.'

'Somewhat. Unfortunately I don't believe you.'

'Nor would the police believe the truth.'

'Is that why you're not going to them?'

'No, not really.'

'You're afraid of talking, then?'

'I'm afraid of nothing, Mr. Flute.'

She turned on me and her eyes were flashing angrily. For a moment she scared me. I realized that this was a woman who could take care of herself, most of the time anyway.

'You'll have to excuse me,' she said, 'I have a photographic session in twenty minutes and have to leave soon.'

She side-stepped me and led the way back to the front door. She had nice legs, solid little thighs, well-kept hands, there was nothing I could object to but her rough treatment of me, but maybe I was just feeling sensitive.

Outside in the windy street I paused to think about the interview. It hadn't got me far, but it had told me that she was scared. I knew, if she didn't, that she needed protection. I hailed a taxi and gave the agency's address.

★ ★ ★

I arrived at North Park Lane House at a quarter to two. I wasn't very surprised to see a policeman at the main entrance but was a little sad to see Fred Scatzikiforijikc being led away by Chaucer. This I observed from a cleaner's cupboard into which I quickly hid as the procession came down the corridor from the studio.

'I am only going to answer a few questions,' Fred was heard explaining to his cheering layout artists. No doubt this would mean a day off for them.

In Bedlington's office I sat down behind his desk and tried to work out a plan of action. The one person I wanted to contact was Lardvik, and I wasn't too sure how to go about it. Then the telephone rang.

'Yes?' I said.

'Is Mr. Lardvik there please?' The voice was agitated.

'No.'

'Have you any idea where he might be? The Chamble Creative Presentation is starting in two minutes and no one has seen him!'

The girl rang off leaving me with a cold receiver. It was odd that Lardvik had got lost on such an important day as this. On the Chamble Creative Presentation depended a vast percentage of the agency's income for the following year. With one managing director dead it was essential that the only other should preside. I decided to investigate.

In the Bedlington, Lardvik Advertising Ltd. reception room some thirty people had gathered. They were an assorted lot, both young and old, some obviously incredibly intelligent, some obviously incredibly stupid.

'How's your head, darling?' A soft, warm voice whispered in my left ear.

'Better for seeing you.'

I took Susan's hand and squeezed it a little. A few feet behind her was the tall blonde man with the curling beard and shining blue eyes.

'When did he turn up?'

'Just now, with me. We had a late lunch.'

I said nothing but looked at Lardvik looking at me. He seemed to be a good actor, he seemed not to recognize me, which was hard to believe with the bruise down the left side of my lovely face.

'Shall we go in?' he said to someone, and a young man in drain-pipe trousers rushed to open the double doors that led to the boardroom.

As we entered, some haunting refrain reached our ears from nowhere. We sat down round a long rectangular table with neatly arranged pencils and paper, glasses, water decanters before each seat.

The carpet was burgundy, the walls dove-grey and the ceiling, very low, was made of sound-proof blocks. Now and again a beam of bright yellow light came down to shine on one of the client's heads, like a ray of sunshine. It was ingenious and awe-inspiring.

When we had all sat down and I had had a good look round to see who was there, I realized that the table arrangement was so worked out that the clients sat on one side facing a specially designed panelled wall, while the agency staff sat on the other. I, of course, had sat on the clients' side opposite Susan who was all smiles, pleased that I was there and begging with her eyes to know where I had been since I had last seen her.

Once everyone had settled down and the double doors had been closed, Francis Gear stood up and clutched his left lapel. As soon as he started to speak the music died down.

'Gentlemen, my name is Francis Gear, and I am the Account Executive on Chamble.' No one clapped, but then no one was supposed to. A girl in a corner, however, scribbled like crazy. 'The music which you have just heard is the proposed backing to the new colour 60-second spot for cinema screen. If I may refer you to the media schedule in front of you, you will see that we propose booking you screening time in forty-two areas over the British Isles from the months of May to September.'

Everyone, including myself, busily looked through the papers to find the Media Schedule. To me it was as understandable as a French menu.

'What about October to April then? Doesn't anyone have a bath in the winter in England?' This upstart was from Bolton, the Sales Manager for the North who was regarded as a bit of a card anywhere else but London.

Francis Gear, with professional aplomb, smiled a resigned smile, making it quite clear that humorous remarks were not appreciated at these sort of meetings. By pressing a button on a small board in front of him he plunged the room into subtle darkness and pressed another to slide open the panelled wall.

A small white screen came to life with a blaze of colour. Reds, mauves, pinks and blues, all bubbles out of focus. The camera panned back and there, looking absolutely delicious immersed in her three feet of foam, was a very pretty girl who seemed to be enjoying every moment of her bath. The background music swelled, the beat increased, and then it was all over.

The lights came on as subtly as they had gone off, the panels closed and everyone turned to hear what Francis Gear had to say next.

'That was the 60-second spot for the summer adapted from a revolutionary 120-second spot for the winter . . . '

He went on about media schedules some more, mentioned a few outrageously unknown areas in Northern Ireland as being good test ground and eventually the lights went down as we watched a longer version of what we had already seen. As the girl lifted a silky white leg, I felt a jab at my ankle.

While all the staff of the agency were looking over their shoulders at the film, young Susan wasn't. She was looking at me and raising her eyebrows. Her toe slowly but surely edged up my leg and stopped short of the knee, only because had she tried to go further she would have slid under the table.

Gear's little lecture lasted half an hour during which we saw three more commercials and two press advertisements. Every time the lights went low Susan dug her toe into my leg, and by the time I had seen the seventh variation of a 15-second television spot, I was playing the same game only my leg stretched much farther.

It was when the managing director of Chamble got up to make a few points that the meeting became really interesting. Among many other criticisms of the campaign he wanted to know why a new girl had been chosen to model in the bath without him being notified. There was a revered hush and Lardvik coughed and looked at Gear.

Gear did not stand up but leaned across the table and in a voice which was loud enough for everyone to hear, but had the reverence of a whisper, he explained calmly that Clementine, who had been in the original films, had refused to do any more modelling for the agency, and as they had only got half-way through the scheduled advertisements they had had to get a new girl.

'Why did she refuse?'

'We don't know,' said Gear in a much quieter voice. 'Mr. Bedlington handled her.'

I thought it was an unfortunate turn of phrase but it did convey exactly what had happened.

The client could do nothing. The fact that Bedlington was dead was a subject which so far had not been brought up.

'I think, however, Francis,' the managing director said, 'we would like to see the first take you did using Clementine. There was something about her which evoked the sort of feeling we want people to associate with Chamble. This new girl is too . . . too . . . '

'Willing?' I suggested.

All eyes turned on me. I was sitting on the wrong side of the table for a start and I wasn't supposed to be there anyway, but the remark went down well with the client. I felt the managing director of Chamble was going to propose me a rise for such lucidity.

'That sums it up very neatly, young man, very neatly.'

Gear, who was considering whether I should be thrown out or not, now played with his button panel and a telephone. After very little time, the room went dark again and the screen came to life.

The film was like the others with perhaps subtler shades of bubbles and smoother music. When the camera panned back we saw a different girl in the bath, older, more mature, a girl who knew exactly what it was all about. Clementine not only made one want to buy Chamble, she made one want to get right into the bath with her.

I was watching closely at the end of the sequence to see if she would step out and reveal anything she shouldn't, when I caught sight of her left hand. Threaded firmly on one of her fingers was Bedlington's signet ring.

I sat perfectly still as Gear got up to talk about the advertising spaces the agency had booked for Chamble in the two Outdoor magazines *Camp Yourself* and *Outdoor Playtime Weekly*. All the attention of the room was focussed on him allowing me to concentrate on my own thoughts without missing anything vital.

So Clementine was one of Bedlington's girls, *the* girl probably since she had worn his ring. Lardvik had this curious relationship with Ninette, and also with Susan. I wondered what it was about the advertising business that made these men get so involved.

With an idea about leaving the board meeting to contact Clementine and make her talk, I looked around to see if anyone would miss me. The next time the lights went down I intended getting out.

But the lights did not go down. Immediately after Gear had finished speaking, the Chamble managing director rose unexpectedly and made an impromptu but startling speech.

Every one was naturally disturbed by the circumstances of Henry Bedlington's death, but with all the will in the world he could not understand why it should have affected an advertising campaign which had started six months ago, nor why Clementine Deshalles should have broken her contract, nor for that matter how the agency had managed to let Cordite Advertising know their plans so that 'Barfnite Ltd' could virtually profit by Chamble's advertising.

I only realized the importance of what had been said when everyone on the agency side of the table turned pale. Were they going to lose the account? Were they all liable to be fired. All eyes turned to Julius Lardvik.

Slowly, uncertainly, Lardvik got up and faced the grim, but satisfied, faces of his clients.

'I think I can explain the three points you have raised with one answer, sir. Miss Clementine Deshalles was the person responsible for leaking our creative ideas to Cordite Advertising.'

The collective gasp paralysed the room for quite some time. The agency side of the table were as shocked as the Chamble side, and I was surprised myself.

Of course it all fitted into place now. The note in the bath, obviously planted by Lardvik, had had nothing to do with the murder at all. *Careless Talk Costs Lives* . . . .Maybe your living . . . was the message intended. He had chosen a slightly violent method of showing he meant business, but then I didn't know Clementine. I breathed a sigh of relief, though it left Ninette's disappearance completely baffling.

'Have you proof of this, Lardvik?' The Chamble managing director asked, quite rightly.

'Among us, gentlemen,' said Lardvik full of confidence, 'is Mr. Flute. A private detective who has been investigating the leak for us. You may ask him any questions you wish.'

A quick, desperate glance from Lardvik told me the whole story. He was passing the buck and begging me to clear the agency's name somehow. So far he hadn't treated me too kindly, but I didn't have to commit myself. As all eyes turned on me, I smiled and stood up.

'I think you will appreciate, gentlemen, that at this stage I cannot divulge any of my findings. As you will appreciate I am working in close conjunction with Scotland Yard, and as the leakage and Mr. Bedlington's sudden death could be linked, I could not possibly say anything at present.'

The room hummed. Lardvik smiled with satisfaction and scribbled something on a piece of paper. I watched him hand the note to a secretary who brought it round to my side of the table.

It just said *Thank you*, the note, *thank you very much, please meet me in my office immediately after the meeting.*

★　★　★

I had never been in Julius Lardvik's office before and I was pleased to get there a few minutes before him, finding it easier to judge a man's character knowing what surroundings he lives in.

I expected to see a fair amount of white wood, a few snowscapes, a stuffed polar bear perhaps, but found myself in a far more chi-chi atmosphere. The layout of the office was similar to Bedlington's though a little smaller. The walls were papered in black and white regency stripes, the floor was carpeted in olive green and most of the furniture was good reproduction Sheraton. There were a number of unknown old masters, heavy green velvet curtains draped across the windows and a marble bust of Bernadotte on a pedestal. I was as impressed as I was meant to be.

The door opened and Lardvik came in. He was smiling as though he had just been told a funny story, went straight to his desk and sat down, suggesting I should do likewise.

'You really must excuse me, but I do not know your first name,' he said, offering me a cigarette.

'Adam,' I said bringing out my lighter.

'Adam Flute. I must congratulate you on handling a very tricky situation. I obviously misjudged you when I first met you at Ninette's. You know, by the way, that she has disappeared?'

'Yes.'

'You don't know where she is?'

'No.'

'Well, anyway, I did not ask you to

come here to discuss that. I still need your help, as you can well imagine.'

I said nothing but examined my nails. They were clean so I looked at him instead.

'As you know,' he said, sitting forward in his chair, awkwardly, making the whole situation an ordeal for both of us, 'As you know, I was not too fond of the idea of you roaming around the agency. But now you could be very useful to me.'

'I'm glad,' I said. I was rubbing the side of my face to let him know that he had been in my mind too.

'We have started this story about Clementine Deshalles being guilty of the leak — and we must end it as diplomatically as possible.'

'Before she starts suing you for slander.'

'Yes.'

'Have you any ideas?' I asked.

'Yes, I have. I would suggest that you told everyone you were wrong. It would be acceptable that you should make an error in your investigations — more acceptable that is than me accusing someone outright.'

'Would it? I don't think it would be to me. I have my reputation to keep, Mr. Lardvik. And I've never made a mistake yet.'

'You would be well paid.'

'Like last night?'

He looked at me bewildered. It was a good act, but I sat and waited a few seconds before applauding.

'I'm sorry, I don't understand you.'

'Last night, Miss Trevelyan's flat, remember?'

He was really puzzled. He was looking at the bruise with some distaste but obviously intrigued.

'Where were you last night, Mr. Lardvik?'

'In Whitstable. I dined with the manager of Instant Oysters Ltd., a new account.'

'You went by car?'

'Yes.'

'Of course.'

'But you didn't stay there very late?'

'I stayed the night. But why?'

'I saw your car parked in Hammersmith at 11 p.m.'

'You couldn't have done. There are quite a lot of black and grey Humbers around you know.'

'I was talking of your blue Rolls-Royce, Mr. Lardvik.'

'Mine? That's not my car. That belonged to Henry Bedlington.'

8

In the majority of advertising agencies the top creative people are plagued by their non-artistic superiors who always think that their own ideas are more original; this is why there is such a high turnover of staff in the advertising business. Everyone hates everyone else's guts.

Lardvik was sitting well back in an armchair opposite me, and we were both smoking cigars and sipping a very good whisky which he had produced from his Sheraton cabinet.

Faced with the fact that the person who had sapped me the night before could not possibly have been Lardvik, I had rapidly changed course. There were few people I could trust now and Susan definitely was not one of them. Taking the opportunity of learning more about the agency intrigues I had asked him to give me the complete breakdown on the 'ideas leak' for which I had originally been hired.

As far as I could gather nothing very unusual had happened except that Henry Bedlington had hired me to expose the matter in order to fire a certain member of the staff he particularly disliked.

'Who?' I asked drawing on my rich Havana and blowing out an elliptical smoke ring.

'I don't suppose you know him.'

'Try me.'

'A man called Fred Scatzikiforijikc.'

'Why should Bedlington sort him out?'

'Fred hated Henry, hated the name Bedlington.'

'Any particular reason?'

'Fred started as a free-lance artist. He worked up in Streatham by himself and got a few clients — hairdressers, the odd restaurant, you know. He was a talented man — I use the past tense deliberately — and had plenty ideas.'

Coming from Julius Lardvik, who had the reputation of being pretty hot on ideas, this was a compliment.

'One day,' he continued, 'the managing director of some chain stores in the north saw his work and was so impressed that he backed him. Fred started his own small agency with a few employees and later, when he had about twenty-five reliable clients, engaged the services of one Henry Bedlington. Henry took everything.'

'How?'

'Used his influence. Overpowered Fred, told him he was a brilliant artist but not a business man and made himself a partner. The union lasted three months then Henry convinced Fred that Scatziki-forijikc & Bedlington Advertising didn't sound too good to the British clients' ears and suggested Bedlington Advertising instead. He was a brilliant salesman.'

'So it seems.'

'Shortly afterwards Bedlington moved the agency to bigger premises, here in fact, and I joined the firm as a partner.'

'Why did he accept you? It sounds as though he might have done quite well on his own.'

'He needed the money and money comes from big accounts. I left my last agency with three such clients, Chamble among them.'

'And Bedlington just wanted to get rid of Fred . . . because he was a nuisance?'

'More or less. Some people grow with an agency, others stay put. Fred hasn't grown.'

'And I was hired purely to cause a scandal so that he could have a good reason to sack him?'

'Yes.'

It was a pleasant story. I had heard that agency men were three-ulcer men with four-ulcer jobs, now I knew why.

'What of Susan Trevelyan?' I asked.

'Susan?' Lardvik smiled. 'You're not bad at your job, not bad at all. Susan was Fred's first secretary. She was with him up in Streatham and he used her as his first model. At one time there was a rumour that they were going to get married, but it fell through.'

'Do you think that Fred Scatz might be involved in Henry Bedlington's murder?'

Things were moving rapidly up there in my mind. Susan tied up with Fred, Fred hating Bedlington's guts . . . girl covers up for male friend. There was a story and a motive here all right.

'Having slandered Miss Deshalles, I can hardly start accusing Fred Scatz of murder. But I wouldn't disagree with the possibility.'

'It wouldn't solve the Ninette disappearing trick though, would it?'

'It might. Fred hated the Bedlingtons. Ninette knew something perhaps?'

He was looking at me over his glass, watching my reaction, seeing if I was believing him. I did believe him quite a bit, but I wasn't cancelling him off my suspect list just yet.

'Have you got his address?'

'Fred's, yes, but why?'

'I'd like to go and see him.'

'But he's been arrested — didn't you know?'

I pretended I didn't. In fact I had forgotten. It was strange that I had singled him out to send to Bowels. There was a chance he was still being held, but I knew the police would stick to the man-in-the-garden-story and he would soon prove his innocence on that score.

I finished my whisky, stubbed out my cigar butt and got up to go.

'Are you really Ninette's godfather?' I asked.

'Yes.'

'You introduced her to Henry Bedlington presumably.'

'Yes.'

'Then those photographs you took of her were posed for before she met him?'

'What photographs?'

'The ones of Ninette in the nude.'

He was not amused. He sat up and narrowed his eyes and stared at me with what some people might have called intense dislike.

'Where did you see those?'

'Someone showed them to me.'

'Everard Philbear?'

'Yes. How did you guess?'

'That's all I could expect from a man like that! He worked quite a lot for this agency before I came. I got rid of him. That was his revenge.'

'The taking of the photographs or saying that you had taken them?'

'Both.'

'But you must admit that Ninette must be quite a flighty bit . . . '

'I must admit nothing, Flute, nothing at all!'

As I left Lardvik in his regency surroundings I realized for the first time that he was not the man I had thought him. He had not taken nude snaps of Ninette, he had not been involved with Susan. A strange, tall, healthy Swede with blond hair and blue eyes. His motives for murdering people would be complicated indeed.

* * *

Fred Scatz was home when I called on him just after eight. A bachelor, he lived in a basement flat in Streatham. He could afford better but he had lived there for a long time and the rent was so low that it was worth the discomfort of never seeing the sun for the amount of money saved.

Fred was very unhappy and basically unlucky. He had been married once, a very long time ago before he came to England, but that was past history. Also in his past history was the fact that he had worked out in Peru which accounted for the living-room walls being covered with Peruvian mementos. Mats, shields, swords, various conical hats and masks of warfare.

At our first meeting he had invited me to call whenever I could spare the time, so he was not particularly surprised to see me. He was starting his dinner and he asked me to join him.

I couldn't remember when I had last eaten and as there was no better place to discuss the past, present and future than over a meal, I accepted.

He was eating liver-sausage and braised leeks helped down with a glass of sweet white wine to which he added a small spoonful of Andrews Liver Salts — this, he admitted, was a cheap way of drinking champagne, but he liked it.

I declined the spoonful of salts on the grounds that I didn't like the idea. He wasn't vexed, it took all sorts to make a world.

By the time we had finished the main dish and were chewing at an old piece of seed cake which he insisted I should eat with my gorgonzola, we had run through the part of his life which Lardvik had traced over for me. It was over the coffee, which was excellent, that I asked him the questions I had come to ask.

It was not hard to get him onto the subject of Bedlington, Lardvik Advertising Ltd., and his venom and hatred of both men soon came out.

The fact that he had been manhandled by the police in the morning and that Lardvik had done absolutely nothing to assist him didn't help the situation. Inspector Bowels had accused him of being in someone's garden somewhere near Primrose Hill the night before and he had not been released till proof of his innocence had shown up in the shape of a forty-five-year-old mistress with whom he had been canoodling. The whole affair had been most humiliating and he wasn't likely to forget it in a hurry.

We moved from the steaming, garlic-smelling kitchen to the Peruvian living-room and I admired the knick-knacks. We sat down in very uncomfortable chairs and I started talking about the murder.

He had no definite ideas about it, he

knew that a number of people would have liked to see him accused, he thought Lardvik a hot favourite — or possibly Everard Philbear.

I was curious at the mention of this name again. Lardvik hadn't talked of the photographer in the kindest of terms, and now Fred was gunning for him.

Everard, to Scatz's mind, was a bit of an amateur who had been lucky. He was an excellent contact man who couldn't be trusted, and as far as killing Bedlington, of course he hadn't only been on the scene of the crime, but also had a motive.

'What?'

'Clementine. A model. Actress she calls herself, but she can't act to save her life. She and Bedlington were hitting it off — and Everard had his eye on her. Besides, Everard's the man who gave all that information to Cordite Advertising.'

Suddenly I could see the whole of my future mapped out clear for me. I would spend the rest of my days interviewing the members of the agency staff and each of them would accuse another and send me off on a wild goose chase.

'I was told you had something to do with the leaking information.'

'Me? Why me? I was the man who had the ideas!'

He shrugged his shoulders, opened a cupboard door of the sideboard and brought out a bottle sheathed in wicker-work.

'Cordite might have offered you money for the information.'

'Money? Do I look like a man who likes money? I live alone, I have few vices most of which are cheap. No . . . Everard is your man if you are hunting for the informer, and if you are looking for a murderer, he might not be a bad bet — but don't ask me how he did it!'

'What about Susan Trevelyan?'

He was pouring this clear gut-rotting liquid into two tiny glasses and he made sure that I wouldn't see his eyes. By the tone of his voice I guessed he was feeling emotional at the sound of her name.

'Susan was my secretary a long time ago. It was I who helped her become the woman she is to-day. I am very fond of Susan, but she is not a very good girl. You can be sure that she is involved in all this business one way or another. She couldn't stay away from anything as exciting as this.'

He handed me my small glass and gave me a lecture on the liquid's origin. It came from Peru like the shields and the masks, and it had something to do with poppy seeds which, if drunk in sufficient quantity, eventually make you sterile. I thanked him very much and set the glass aside.

'You knew that Ninette Bedlington had disappeared?'

'That's what the police arrested me for.'

'Of course. You have no ideas about where she might be?'

He swallowed his glassful in one gulp and helped himself to another dram.

'Ninette? She's pretty friendly with Everard. Probably hiding in his studio!'

9

Outside Scatz's front door, among the dustbins and potted plants and at the foot of the basement steps, I said goodbye to my host and slowly climbed into the murk of a thick granulated grey-green smog.

The day hadn't been too cheerful but now it was damp and filthy and cold. As I walked down the road towards the main Streatham shopping centre I tried not to move my head for fear of getting a black grimy ring round my neck and ruining my shirt collar by rubbing in some of the Greater London grit.

When I reached a cross-roads, with its traffic lights weakly trying to lend colour to the pathetically abysmal scene, I had to be brave. From somewhere I could hear footsteps and also the gentle reassuring hum of a London taxi.

The taxi came into view before the owner of the footsteps and I hailed it. As I got in, I saw the person who had been following me, a man wearing a grey raincoat, a hat and unfortunately a pair of bright yellow gloves. Unfortunately, because the gloves allowed me to recognize him when he got out of another taxi at the corner of Curzon Street where I had decided to alight just to see if I was being followed.

As I walked down Curzon Street, heading in the direction of Everard Philbear's studio, I concentrated on the sounds behind me. The man was wearing ordinary leather-soled shoes, but one of his heels had a metal nail in it; this enabled me to keep track of his movements and verify that he was stopping whenever I stopped.

Curzon Street was brighter than Streatham, the White Elephant Club was bulging out with its usual quota of film producers and starlets and the tall strong doorman was re-directing all the traffic to let a small Rolls Royce park as near the entrance as possible. Further along, the cinema announced its intellectual sex film with tall red neon signs and even further down the smaller neon sign in a private house window advertised French lessons for midnight students.

I stopped outside these three premises and looked around. My companion was still behind me, not in any way attempting to make a good job of his assignment, which, after a moment's thought, sent a shiver down my back. Maybe I was supposed to be frightened, or anyway aware of his presence officially.

I turned into Everard's mews and flattened myself against the door of some elegant greengrocer. Seven seconds later the man with the yellow gloves passed right by me and stopped dead in his tracks.

I couldn't see his face, but I had a feeling he was quite young. He was a bit smaller than me, lighter, not a man I would be frightened of unless he carried a gun. He stayed where he had stopped for some time then moved on a little and quickly darted in another direction.

Diagonally across from my hiding place I could see the door to Everard Philbear's studio. No lights were coming from the premises and I decided that the place was probably empty, but I was amused by the situation and decided to wait a while to see what my friend further down the mews would do.

He was more impatient than I, and after five minutes he popped his head out and looked up the cobbled street. All I wanted was to know what he looked like; maybe he was a policeman, maybe Bowels had had me tailed for days, but I felt that this was no professional and guessed that his assignment was definitely not a happy one.

As he started walking towards me I stepped quickly back into the shadows. Now I had the chance of finding out who it was, if I was fool enough to show myself. But I let him go. I was the one that was being hunted and at this stage of my young career I didn't relish the thought of going around with bits of lead in my stomach.

When the coast was clear I ran down the mews in the opposite direction and in the main road hailed a cab, got in and gave the driver my home address. I had

had a hard day, a large helping of liver
sausage and leeks and a long walk in the
fog. I deserved a rest. I snuggled into the
cold corner of the taxi and tried to
remember how many Seltzer tablets I had
left.

★   ★   ★

I sat up in bed, drank my early morning
cup of coffee and read through the file of
Chamble copy which had supposedly
been leaked through to Cordite Advertising Ltd. My attention was caught by such
arresting statements as:

*Chamble Is Better Than A Wash
— It Frees You From Personal Dirt!*
*Bubble Your Way To His Arms in
Dreamy Chamble Soap Suds.*
*More Exhilarating Than A Cold
Shower — Piping Hot Chamble.*
*Be Sure You Have A Clean Face In
Front Of That Dirty Mind.*
*Mermaids In The Bahamas Swear
By It!!!*

The telephone rang. I picked up the dusty receiver and listened.

'I'd like to see you as soon as possible,' she said. It was Clementine Deshalles afraid of something.

'Name the place and time,' I said.

'Can you meet me at the film studios? Merton Park, Stage 3. I'm doing a commercial there at ten-thirty.'

I said I would and hung up. My interest in Chamble baths got lost as I got up and opened my wardrobe to choose a suitable suit to meet Miss Deshalles. Of all the girls I had met during my Bedlington campaign, she was the one who had excited my sense of values most. She seemed unattainable and played hard to get, she knew what men wanted and wasn't going to give it to them too easily.

I chose my check suit with the drainiest of drainpipe trousers; with it I could wear my soft suede shoes which allowed me to pad around places noiselessly. Thinking of padding around reminded me of old Yellow Gloves the night before and I took a look out of the window at the street below and the park beyond. There was no one around acting suspiciously, all I was aware of was the beautiful poetic mist clinging romantically to the trees which I knew perfectly well was the filthy fog of the night before.

*　　*　　*

Putney Heath had its own ration of fog and I was allowed a visibility of about fifty yards, which meant I couldn't drive as fast as my car wanted. I found Merton Park Studios sandwiched between houses in a suburban street and didn't hide my disappointment. Film studios to me brought visions of tall guarded gates, palm trees, huge white hangars, a couple of blue swimming pools with furniture and female fittings, maybe a bar or two, glamour anyway. Instead I found myself looking at a couple of old warehouses, a sour old doorman with a uniform round his body and doubt in his mind as to my acceptability.

I asked for Clementine Deshalles, told him she was on Stage 3, made a lot of fuss, troubled him no end till he realized it would be easier for him to let me in than find the person who had asked me up.

I went down an unheated corridor, turned left, then right, found a thick door, pulled it open and stepped into the warm arc-lamp-lit studio.

The setting seemed to be for some kind of cannibal ritual. I couldn't complain any more, there were more palm trees per square foot than in any self-respecting jungle, and in the clearing, lying on some straw, was Clementine herself.

She was dressed in bright orange pants and a black short-sleeved sweater. One leg was lying flat, the other was artistically flexed. Her hands were folded behind her head and she had her mouth wide open.

Four feet above her, a small man with close-cropped hair was dangling a long piece of chocolate from an invisible thread. The idea being to drop the chocolate into her mouth.

A crowd of twenty technicians were watching this delicate performance and one of them whispered in my ear that she had now eaten seventeen of the chocolates and nearly choked twice. The cameraman was having an argument with the producer and under the arc lamps the supply of chocolates was slowly but surely melting.

'We'll try it once more. O.K., Clementine love?'

The technicians got to their positions and as the camera started whirring the close-cropped man, who was only paid thirty-five pounds a week for this job, expertly lowered the chocolate into Clementine's mouth. It missed.

By the time they had taken nine shots of this sequence and Clementine had got up and dusted her back, combed her hair, re-adjusted her face, I had taken a seat in the shadow of a palm tree and was having a gentle conversation about advertisements with an accounts executive from Cordite Advertising Ltd. He was taking some pains to explain that romance and chocolates went together. Market Research teams had proved without a doubt that sucking chocolates and kissing gave a girl exactly the same sensation, which didn't worry me a bit till he offered me a Looloobell Pencil Bar — 'The chocolate that's the same size as your pencil!'

Clementine came off the set, saw me under my palm tree and sauntered towards me. She smiled as though I were some old acquaintance and made me understand by a quick glance that we couldn't talk here.

The man from Cordite was only just polite to her. He was, it appeared, her employer for the day and he was pretending that he wasn't satisfied with her performance. Knowing how much she was being paid by the agency, Clementine took all his insults calmly and when he finally left us to pick an argument with the producer she just shrugged her shoulders.

'Someone has been following me for the last two days, and I don't like it,' she said.

'Like you didn't like your brother's party?'

'Just like that. We can't talk here because I'm being watched by someone who knows us both, a person who I think has a fair amount to do with this whole business.'

'What business are we talking about, leaks or murder?'

She tightened the wide belt round her thin waist and stared across the studio floor. Standing in the doorway was a familiar figure, a person I badly wanted to question, Susan Trevelyan herself.

'Is she your suspect?' I asked.

'Maybe.'

At that precise moment the Cordite man came hurrying back and grabbed hold of Clementine's arm.

'We'll have to do that shot again, you had your left leg up instead of your right.'

'After lunch, my place,' Clementine said over her shoulder.

I nodded. I had other things to keep me busy, too, and I didn't want to lose sight of Susan.

As I made my way round the back of the scenery, picking my path through bits of plastic jungle, stuffed tigers, two elephants tusks and empty bottles of beer, some agitated young man in a polo-neck sweater stopped me.

'Have you seen her white poodle?'

'Whose? Clementine's?'

'Yes!'

'No.'

'I've got to find it! She asked me to look after it and it got out of her dressing room.'

The white poodle was found under one of the arc lamps licking all the melted Looloobell Pencil Bars. Susan Trevelyan, however, couldn't be found anywhere.

I didn't bother to search the Merton Park area for the blonde, but took a spin down to my uncle's club to have a cheap read through the morning papers. Every one of them lied about Bedlington's murder and Ninette's disappearance except *The Times*, which didn't mention the affair at all. I knew that the one person who could tell me everything was Susan, but I also knew that she wouldn't be an easy person to corner. I had a couple of drinks in the bar and then headed for Clementine's apartment.

As before, I had no difficulty in getting to the place, through the front door and up to the second floor, nor did I have any difficulty in getting into the flat. Pressing the bell next to the front door I realized that again it was not closed and by gently pushing it a little I found myself standing inside the small hall, warm and scented.

There was no one in the living-room, no one in the kitchen, no one in the bath or the bathroom but in her bedroom I found her little white poodle sitting and panting nervously in the middle of her well-upholstered double bed.

At first I didn't think anything of it. She might have come in, in a hurry, and gone out to get some cigarettes or a drink. On the other hand she might never have come in at all. The latter thought entered my head when I noticed the pair of gloves next to the poodle. They were yellow.

Aware suddenly that Clementine might be in trouble I turned round to leave the flat, but didn't get very far. Standing in the doorway, barring any hurried exit I might have contemplated, was Susan gripping an ugly, black Mauser.

The front door was now closed, there was about four feet between us and she was leaning comfortably against the frame of the bedroom door.

'It's not loaded of course?' I said playfully.

'Like a bet?'

Her hand was remarkably steady and she had a charming smile. I was trying to gauge her mood but found the going hard. I wasn't dealing with a voluptuous blonde any more, but a lively animal who had the upper hand of a tricky situation and who knew more about my position in it than I did.

'How long have you been following me, then?' I asked.

'Shall we move to the living-room?'

She was backing into the hall to give me plenty of room to do as she had asked. I had no option and didn't right then feel like dying or even being crippled. I led the way into the living-room like a good boy and waited for further instructions.

'Perhaps it wasn't you, but your mate. Though he did look pretty effeminate come to think of it.'

'Sit down please.'

She had no respect for me any more, I could tell. I watched her move across the room, still pointing the lethal weapon in my direction, and sit down on a chair near the desk. With her free hand she reached for the telephone and picked up the receiver.

'Ringing up the police?' I asked.

Keeping her eyes on me she managed to dial the number she wanted and waited patiently for the other end to answer.

'If you shoot me, the police will get you, you know. You haven't a hope of getting out of this one. Was it you who killed Bedlington?'

She didn't say anything but kept a steady eye on me, a steady finger on the trigger and a steady ear to the receiver.

'Hallo?' she said at last. 'It's Susan. I've got him.'

The reaction on her face told me that someone at the other end was paying her compliments. I could hear a mumbling coming from the receiver but nothing was very distinct. She said a 'yes' a couple of 'no's', nodded her head once or twice but gave nothing away. After a while longer she smiled an unpleasant smile and hung up. I knew that someone, somewhere, had decided my fate.

'You are taking me for a ride,' she said at last, getting to her feet. 'I want you to walk out of this flat and down to your car and drive me where I tell you without making any attempts at getting the better of me.'

I looked at the little black hole at the end of the Mauser, thought about the little piece of well-shaped lead that might come out of it and shrugged my shoulders like any intelligent hero would.

Slowly I walked towards the door. It was a ridiculous situation to be in and one I knew I couldn't tolerate. If I didn't spring a fast one on her soon, things wouldn't be in my favour any more. Outside in the street the chances were that she might hurt someone else, and I couldn't risk that — I was a decent chap.

The open door leading to the hall was in front of me, Susan with the gun behind me slightly to my right. I moved slowly towards the doorway then, as she took a step, I hurled myself onto the floor into the hall, rolled to my left and crouched just inside the bedroom.

I waited there holding my breath. If she shot at me she couldn't possibly hit me from where she was, and she wouldn't dare move, not knowing whether I was armed or not. I was happy in my new position, she would be rattled and it would make her realize how vulnerable she was.

'I forgot to tell you, Adam,' she said in that deep melancholic voice of hers, 'that if you don't drive me where I ask you to, and if we don't get to that destination by a certain time, Clementine Deshalles will suffer.'

It wasn't a bad plan at all. It was so good in fact that it allowed her to stand in the doorway looking down at me without even aiming her gun. There was absolutely nothing I could do and she knew it.

'What if I don't care about Clementine?' I said, getting up and dusting myself.

'But you do care. You care a lot. She's young and beautiful.'

We left the apartment in a hurry and

went peaceably down in the lift.

It was marvellous really. I was being kidnapped possibly on the strength of a great big hoax. For all I knew Clementine might be dead. But I couldn't risk a life, not on my own. I had decided to work alone and this was the penalty.

As we walked to my car she explained quite calmly that she would tell me where to go and that I was to do just as she said. She had no idea what was in store for me, but she was sure that the person she was working for wouldn't hurt me more than was necessary. After all, I wasn't the law, and I was in the detective business for money. Maybe an arrangement could be made.

We both got into the car normally and I started up the engine. I was pleased that the smog was coming down again, it gave me the feeling that it might be a good excuse for not going where she wanted me to, or something.

As I headed towards Chelsea she told me to get onto the Great West Road. She lit me a cigarette, switched on the wireless and suggested I should enjoy the drive since there was nothing I could do about it. However cosy she made me feel she carefully avoided answering any of my questions.

At a roundabout she told me to head for Richmond. With luck I realized I might have the whole journey mapped out for me, all I needed was a good memory to remember the road signs. We might be going to Wales.

Round Weybridge, however, we started taking odd little turnings and by the tone of her voice I knew we were near our destination. When we turned into St. George's Hill, which I knew to be a stockbrokers' paradise and a maze of little lanes, huge houses punctuated occasionally by the odd golf course and swimming pool, she switched off the radio and concentrated on the road ahead.

She made me turn left, then right, then left again and when I nearly swerved off the road altogether she suggested I should switch on my lights. It was around four now and quite dark with the fog adding charm to the whole proceedings.

Suddenly she told me to turn down a

very narrow lane and I plunged the car into the depths of an overgrown wood, down a track which came to a surprising dead end.

This was apparently it. We both got out of the car and she brought out her little black Mauser again to remind me that this was no picnic. We walked up a steep hillock then down again into a forest of blackleaved rhododendron bushes. The air was damp and cold and underfoot the sodden earth cracked with rotting branches and decaying leaves. It was an ideal place for a party.

Suddenly a very tall man appeared in front of us, and to make me feel welcome, he shone his big bright torch straight into my face before turning round to lead the way to wherever my captors had decided to take me.

I had never seen the man before, but his size was impressive enough for me to know that I wouldn't find it easy to escape from him if he was to act as my guard.

The whole area of the wood was not probably very big but it was a good spot to hide someone — right in the middle of civilisation yet far from the passing crowds. Weybridge was a respectable area, St. George's Hill even more so — until now.

We reached a clearing and I saw the roof of a wooden hut the size of a large summer house. It was there, at the top of some steps leading down to the hut, that Susan hit me.

She hadn't the strength or the experience to hit me properly the first time, so she had to hit me again. It was painful and it made me taste blood. Slowly, as I saw the huge form of her friend loom up over me, I was enveloped in the soft woolly black cloud of pain and unconsciousness.

My coma didn't last long. Even Susan's second attack hadn't worked too well, though it had given me enough of a headache to make me lie absolutely still and yearn for some of the agency's sea-sickness tablets.

Two people were carrying me, not with great ceremony, and all I could do was pretend that I didn't know. A door creaked open and I felt a wave of warmth and smelt the smarting smell of paraffin. Then the big man spoke unexpectedly.

'He's pretending,' he said. 'I'll have to 'it 'im again.'

Which he did, with surprising skill, for I only woke up again some five hours later.

10

I opened my eyes and saw nothing. I batted my eyelids, felt my face, but still I could see nothing. I reached a little to my left and took her hand, a soft, small, cool hand, which had been soothingly rubbing the side of my head where it hurt most, but still I could see nothing.

'Are you awake?' It was a beautifully clear voice in the darkness and I ran my hand up her naked arm to touch the gentle line of her chin and lips.

'Yes,' I said in a choked voice. Any slight move on my part brought a jab of pain right down the back of my neck.

'Is it dark in here or have I gone blind?'

'No, there is no light at all.'

I took a deep breath and put my hands firmly down on the ground beneath me. The concrete floor seemed to be covered by some sort of matting. I eased myself up and leaned against the wall.

'It is you, Clementine, isn't it?' I wasn't

sure who the girl was except that she seemed unexpectedly friendly.

'Yes.'

'Where are we and how long have we been here?'

'We're in a sort of shelter. I've been here some time, a day anyway. I've lost count. You were brought in here about five hours ago.'

'Who by?'

'Susan and Big Harry.'

It didn't mean anything to me. I hadn't the faintest idea what she was talking about and I don't know that right then I cared. By groping my hand round in the dark I had come to the conclusion that she was wrapped up in some sort of blanket but that she was shoeless and that her clothing, if any, was thin.

'What happened to you?' I asked.

'I don't really remember all of it. I left the studio to go back to the flat and Susan offered me a lift. I got into her car and . . . I just don't know. I must have been knocked unconscious.'

'No headache when you woke up?'

'No. But I have a pain in my arm.'

155

'They injected you with something.'

'They? But who?'

'Whoever it is. Do you remember waking up?'

'Yes. I was lying on some sort of camp bed in the middle of this hut. Above us.'

The hut. I remembered the hut now and the drive down, Susan and her plan and the big man. It seemed that the blonde was a professional kidnapper.

'What is this hut, any idea?'

'No. Not really. It was furnished with deck chairs and things, but down here it seems to be quite well planned. It's warm considering the time of year. Maybe it's a sort of fall-out shelter.'

'What's the situation around here, how are we placed?'

'This room is about five foot square. It's got a very low ceiling and a trap door in the far corner. In another corner there's some straw to sleep on. It isn't bad, but I'm a bit cold. They took all my clothes away in case I tried to escape.'

'All your clothes?'

'Well, I've got a slip, but it's hardly enough to keep me warm.'

I said nothing but thought plenty. I closed my eyes, but it made no difference.

'Are there any spiders?' I asked.

It had the desired effect. She was cold anyway and any excuse to get up close to another human being who might emit a little warmth was understandable. I hugged her a bit, forgot my headache and got up enough energy to kiss her. Her mouth, in the black darkness, brought me images of fires and ruby red grottoes shining in the warm mists of a summer's night. After a moment she pulled away remembering that she had been brought up decently.

'Big Harry comes in every two hours,' she said quickly. 'He brings me food. He's a nice man who is obviously being blackmailed to do this job.'

'Probably got a prison record or is hiding from the police.'

Slowly I got to my feet and found that my head just touched the ceiling.

I made a survey of the room feeling everywhere with the tips of my fingers. It was a well-built shelter with a heavy beam in the centre. The exit hatch was fairly large and strongly made of cast iron. A good locking device on the other side would make this a perfect prison. Somewhere there was an air vent, but I couldn't find it, and certainly there was no light coming in.

'You don't suffer from claustrophobia?' I said to make conversation, as I sat down next to her and felt her bare shoulders quite suddenly in the dark.

'Not if I don't think about it.'

'You're very cold. Would you like my coat?'

It was a gentlemanly gesture, the least I could do in the circumstances. I took off my jacket and helped her on with it. As she was now standing up it was a wonderful opportunity to take her in my arms and keep her a little bit warmer. Without her shoes she was really quite small. A tender little bird who knew that life was for living.

'What are we going to do?' she asked after a fair time had elapsed.

'Escape.'

'But how?'

It was a good question and one that

needed a fair amount of thought. They had emptied my pockets of everything and I wondered why they had bothered to leave me my clothes. Perhaps they had been in a hurry.

'Let's sit down a moment and work things out,' I said.

We sat down together in the straw and held each other's hands to keep warm.

'Now then, you rang me up, remember? Why?'

'I thought you could help.'

'Then you knew that this might happen?'

'I felt something might.'

'But who did you fear?'

'That's what I wanted you to find out. After I found my flat was messed up I realized that someone must have wrong ideas about me.'

'What do you mean — wrong?'

'Well, whoever has thought it necessary to kidnap me must think I know something.'

'Don't you?'

'No. What am I supposed to know?'

'Who killed Bedlington.'

She was silent. For the first time I wished there was some light around so that I could study her expression.

'Have you any ideas?' I asked.

'None. It could be anybody. All I know is that it wasn't me.'

'Lardvik?'

'Could be.'

'Everard Philbear?'

'Because of me and Henry you mean? He is a strange boy.'

'Jealousy is a motive.'

'But then he wouldn't act in this way, locking us up together.'

I could see her point. So after all this adventure I wasn't going to find out anything. Someone thought she knew something of importance and maybe she did without realizing it.

'How long were you friends with Henry Bedlington?' I asked.

'Three months. But he got a bit silly and I tried to make a break. He stopped my contract to show me how powerful he was. I couldn't really afford that.'

'You used to wear his signet ring. When did you give it back?'

'The day he broke my contract.'

'When was that?'

'A few days before he was murdered. The last time I saw him . . . we had made it up, we were going out to dinner that night, but he didn't live long enough to make it . . . '

A pattern was beginning to form in my head. A vague idea of what the killer might have tried to do was taking shape in the numbness behind my eyes.

'Was your romance with Bedlington involved?'

'I suppose so.'

'Did most people know about it?'

'Some. Most of the agency staff.'

'Supposing someone had planned to kill Bedlington some time ago — but was waiting for an opportunity to incriminate someone else, could they have chosen your quarrel with him as evidence?'

'Possibly. I was one of the last people to see him.'

A well-planned murder, a person with a natural motive used as a scapegoat, the crime to be discovered by a private eye to muddle the police. Clementine could have been chosen as scapegoat number one, and me as number two. In order to prove my own innocence I should have hunted her out and accused her. It was a good plan but somewhere along the way things had gone wrong. What had Susan to do with all this, and why had Ninette disappeared? Another kidnap? Another murder?

'We've got to get out of here,' I said.

'How?'

As we lay in the straw another little idea formed in my mind. I held her close, so as to get some of the warmth of my coat back, and I told her how I thought we could work an escape. It was all a matter of keeping Big Harry busy when he next came down.

She reckoned that he wouldn't bring her another meal for an hour or so, unless he came down to see how I was getting on, so we just nestled together and enjoyed each other's company as best we could, lying in the straw, in the dark, with her hardly clothed and me well rested after five hours' enforced sleep.

★   ★   ★

Big Harry opened up the trap door half an hour later. The bright light that came pouring in dazzled us both, but we had heard him coming and had had time to take action.

I lay in the same place as I had been put, quite still, holding my breath. Clementine stood up and went towards Big Harry as he came down the steps unsteadily holding a tray on which there were two mugs and two plates of sandwiches.

'Now stand well back, Miss, or I'll have to use force — you know them's me orders.'

'He's dead!' she cried, as I suggested she should.

'He's what?'

Kidnapping and keeping two people out of the way for a while was one thing, but murder was another. Big Harry wasn't very happy.

'Well, he hasn't been breathing and certainly hasn't moved,' went on Clementine breathlessly.

163

'Oh my Gawd.'

As expected Big Harry leaned over me and put a big rough hand heavily on my chest. If my heart was beating he couldn't feel it and I wasn't breathing which was a sure sign of something.

Troubled by the fact that he might have a dead man on his hands he decided to make absolutely sure and picked up my wrist as he had seen doctors do in Emergency Ward 10. While he was concentrating on my apparent lack of life, Clementine quickly, silently, slipped up the steps and out of the black hole.

'I think you're right, Miss . . . ' Big Harry started saying, and when he looked over his shoulder he saw that she was gone.

He let my wrist drop with no thought for me at all and leapt up the steps. As soon as he was gone I stood up and followed cautiously.

Clementine had done the trick. As planned, she had got out, left the hut and would now be hiding somewhere in the bushes. I peeped out of the hole and saw Big Harry standing in the doorway of the little hut. He was hesitating about leaving the place when, again as planned, Clementine screamed from the undergrowth.

Relieved that he hadn't lost his charge Big Harry bolted out into the darkness and I escaped into the night air.

In two bounds I was out of the hut and hiding in the bushes myself. As soon as Clementine saw that I was out, she showed herself.

I doubt whether Big Harry would have got her if she hadn't willingly given herself up, but his heavy gait rushed him to the scene where Clementine had got her slip caught in some brambles.

She had trodden on some thorns, she explained as she let him grab her wrist. Then she supposedly burst into tears at the thought of having to go back into the shelter with a dead man.

Harry understood. He suggested that she should have a cup of tea with him and that she should promise to stay in the hut while he went down and got the dead man out.

Batting her eyelids and promising an

awful lot more, by a smile, a look in her eyes, she watched while Big Harry lowered himself down into the shelter.

By this time I was watching everything through the small latticed window of the hut. As soon as he had disappeared, Clementine slammed down the lid and I leapt in to help.

The struggle he put up was more than I had expected. Being tall, Big Harry had all the strength of his body to push against the lid which we were trying to bolt down on him. For quite a while both Clementine and myself knelt on the cast-iron lid trying to get the locking device into place. Finally I jumped up and landed in the centre of the lid. A cry of agony was muffled as it closed and Clementine slammed the lock shut. His head had taken most of the impact.

With Big Harry out of the way, all we had to do was make our escape before anyone else turned up. It took us a little time to find the path back to where I had parked my car, and with the wet mass of rhododendron bushes and thorny hedges Clementine found the going cold and hard.

Naturally my own car had gone, and I didn't think of stealing one till I saw the back of a gleaming Rover parked in the garage of a rich stockbroker's house. Calling the police, which we could well do, would delay everything and get me involved with Bowels. I suggested to Clementine that we should take a risk and padded round to the front of the house to see if there was any life.

The television was on in the front room and three silhouettes told me the coast couldn't be clearer. The car door was open and I soon found the catch to the bonnet. Clementine watched me with some fascination as I flipped open the fuse box and crossed two of the fuses. A tickle here, a pull there and the engine started.

Clementine leapt in and without any difficulty I drove the car gently down the drive and into the road that would eventually lead us out of St. George's Hill.

As we gathered speed I switched on the lights. If the owner discovered the theft now we might meet some trouble on the way back to London, but with luck he would go on sitting in front of his telly for another hour. The tank was full, the car was in excellent condition, and I did a steady seventy-five on the deserted road.

We reached Bayswater three-quarters of an hour later and I told Clementine to forget her pride and walk boldly into the block of flats dressed as she was.

The sight of a girl in underwear, barefooted, in the middle of winter, did not shock any of the passers-by. The only man in the entrance hall of Porchester Court looked blankly at her not believing his eyes — until he saw me. Then it made sense.

Kitty was busy with her VHF set and I leaned over the counter to whisper in her ear.

'Any Rovers stolen to-night, Kitty?'

'Rovers? Yes!' she said. 'Funny you should ask. One's just been reported missing from the Weybridge area. Grey, registration number R for Romeo, Z for Zooloo, X for X-Ray, seven, one, three.'

'It's outside,' I said. 'I should ring them

up, you might get a reward. While you're at it you might let the owner know that in a hut at the bottom of his neighbour's garden there's a big man who needs feeding every twelve hours.'

I didn't wait to see her expression but joined Clementine in the small lift and pressed the button for the top floor.

11

I showed Clementine into my bedroom, told her to settle down, have a bath, a good rest, help herself to whatever food there was in the fridge but on no account to open any front doors or answer telephones. With her safely in my pyjamas I felt I could go chasing after clues.

Changing into my sleuthiest clothes I took my uncle's Luger from the study desk, made sure it wasn't loaded, and left the flat.

Outside five policemen and two squad cars were busy examining the Rover. There was no doubt in their minds that they had found something of value. I wondered if any of them had been instructed to look for my barouche.

Driving back from Weybridge I had grilled Clementine, I had asked her questions, counter questioned the questions, analysed the answers and had come up with some startling facts. One of them was that I was as perplexed about the whole business as she was, the other was that I had the choice of three suspects, Lardvik, Philbear and Scatz.

Scatz, on intuition, I tended to discard. He had no real motive other than the dislike he had of Bedlington and the set-up — hardly enough reason to kill, let alone plan the killing.

Lardvik was a big mix up — Ninette's godfather, also possibly a photographer of sorts. Maybe a friend of Susan's though his Whitstable story might be true, a man who would gain financially by Bedlington's death, virtually inheriting the agency, and without a doubt in the know about the 'leak' planned by Bedlington to cause a scandal.

Everard Philbear was my hot favourite of the moment, mainly because I knew less about him than the others. There was the story of him being fond of Clementine. He could have taken Ninette's photographs and be involved with her, Scatz had suggested he might be hiding her. He had been having a rough time from Lardvik, maybe also from

Bedlington. The world was full of ugliness and beautiful thoughts. I hailed a clean taxi, and gave the driver Lardvik's home address.

I was going to make a job of it to-night. A round robin of surprise calls. Whoever the criminal was, he didn't think I'd be around, the shock of seeing me might make him drop fresh evidence. The taxi stopped.

Lardvik lived in a studio house just off Hampstead Heath. It was built of bricks and mortar but had an outer coating of white wood to tell everyone that no ordinary person was living there.

The front door was made of glass which allowed everyone to look into the clinically clean hall. Without going in I could see the ladder-like staircase leading to the first floor and the clever way the house was decorated with different shades of blue paint and no furniture whatso-ever. I pressed the bellpush and listened to the sickening chimes of a musical box somewhere near the kitchen.

A door opened and Lardvik appeared. He was in dinner jacket and smoking a cigar, hamming the English gentleman like mad and obviously displeased at seeing my face again.

'Yes?'

He didn't open the glass door wide, he just touched his eyebrows a little and tried a smile.

'I wanted to ask you a few more questions.'

'What about? This is a most inconvenient time, I have guests for dinner.'

'Oh, I thought you were watching television.' I grinned at his dinner jacket, but he didn't appreciate the joke.

'Can't it wait? These are some of my wife's relations and they're only here for a few days. To-morrow, at the office perhaps?'

'You're married?' I said, surprised.

'Yes.'

'I didn't know.'

'To-morrow, at my office?'

'O.K.'

He smiled without effort this time and closed the door after I had walked slowly down the front garden path. I hadn't wasted my time. I had learnt one new angle on Lardvik and I was now confident that he had had nothing to do with Susan's kidnapping me. Everard Philbear was my next call, so I started walking down a narrow hill to the main road where I hoped to get a cab. But I didn't.

It came from behind me, headlights blazing, engine revving. The hill curved quite a bit and the car nearly didn't make it. I stopped as it parked itself two feet from where I was about to step over a drain, both doors swung open and two men got out to bar my way.

'All right, Flute, you're coming with us.'

I didn't argue. One of the men was behind me patting his hands all the way down my body and up again; it didn't take him long to find the Luger and this I knew would be enough to delay me a few weeks.

'I hope it's not loaded, Flute,' Bowels said, showing me into the back seat so that I collided with his partner who was huddled in the other corner.

'I only had it on me to scare someone.'

'You can tell me all about it at the station.'

The other officer, the one who had been making passes at me, got in the front seat and told the driver to move. We reached Bowel's office in just under ten minutes, the man at the wheel was due to be off-duty the moment we arrived.

They made me sit down on a hard stool, but they gave me a cup of tea. They weren't pulling me in on any rap, they just wanted to know what I had been up to, the rough treatment had been to make me talk more easily.

I told Bowels my life story, starting from three days back. I lied a bit here and there, forgot to mention that I had ever met Clementine, talked a fair amount about following shadows down side streets and laid it on pretty thick for old Susan. I knew I'd never find her with my one-man organization, but if they issued a statement to the Press they might get her out into the open.

Bowels asked me why I had visited Lardvik, and I told him. I thought that he might be more involved in the 'leak' than he pretended, and Bowels leaned hard on both his elbows and told me a secret. He, himself, had a feeling. He felt that the 'leak' and the murder might be connected.

I looked at him with fascinated interest and he was very pleased. He made me sign a statement which made me promise I wouldn't interfere any more and then promptly suggested that I should help him.

They were pretty busy chasing up useless clues, the police, and they didn't have any idea who was who or why. It was quite obvious that they had a sneaking admiration for my work, for I was the only one on their side who was right inside the agency, able to work on the staff without arousing suspicion.

My one concern was Ninette, my client. Because of her I agreed to work for Bowels for nothing, that is to say I was considered by them to be nothing more than a nark who would hang around Bedlington, Lardvik Advertising Ltd. till something they thought worth investigating turned up. The option was a few days' detention for carrying a firearm.

Out in the street in the pouring rain I cleared my lungs. Two or three patrol cars were now descending on Susan's flat and every man on the beat would tomorrow be looking out for her. From all the questions Bowels had asked me I had gathered that Ninette's disappearance was still a mystery, but one they did not seem to worry too much about. No girls had been dragged out of the Thames lately, or been reported throttled on Clapham Common.

I walked slowly down Regent Street and took a good long look at the windows which were beginning to show signs of Christmas extravagance. Twelve yards behind me an inconspicuous cop was tailing me, stopping at every street corner to read the sports page of yesterday's evening paper and lighting a cigarette every four puffs. I shook him off by getting onto a No. 12 bus which dropped me at the next traffic lights just as the cop was getting into a cab. I ran down a one-way street and got completely clear of him after doubling back. It took me just under eight minutes to reach Everard Philbear's studio, which, to my satisfaction, showed signs of life.

The fashionable photographer with the blinks had sent his Technicolor secretary home and was, like most of his kind, about to climb up into his bunk-like bed above the studio when I rang the bell.

He wasn't very pleased to see me but he couldn't afford to miss the bit of gossip which I suggested I might tell him about. Having been connected with Bedlington, Lardvik Advertising Ltd., his other clients expected him to know the very latest details.

I followed him up the steep stairs and down into the studio. I sat on a divan which he explained to me was to be reclined on by some notorious actor dressed in 'Over Aereated Underwear' the following morning, and offered me a cup of tea.

'How well do you know Clementine Deshalles?' I asked for a start.

'Why?'

'She's missing.'

'What do you mean?' He was more

concerned than I had anticipated.

'What I said. She's missing, like Ninette. I think both of them have been done in.'

It was the way I put it that did it. He just dropped his cuppa like they do in the films when they've had a shock.

'You're not serious.'

'Very,' I said. My lips were thin and drawn in, I hated breaking bad news to people. I looked away to hide the tears that might be welling up in my eyes. When I looked up he was sitting down on a chair, on the very edge of it, as though he had been hit or something.

'Oh my God,' he said, then after a while: 'Have you told the police?'

'Of course.'

'I'm not the marrying type, Flute, but I would have tried to marry that girl if I had had the chance.'

'It's not certain that she's dead,' I said to make it a little easier for him. 'Besides I thought she was Bedlington's girl.'

'She was, but only for the money. Not that she got paid the way you might think, but . . . well . . . he used her in the ad.

films and they're profitable for an out-of-work actress.'

'You were in love with her?' I asked.

'I suppose so.' He was blinking furiously at the floor now.

'And love and jealousy are motives, Mr. Philbear.'

'I know, I know. That's why I haven't been too co-operative with the police. The moment they tie me up with Clementine and her with Bedlington . . . they'll be round.'

The thought didn't attract him and I watched him open the drawer of some chest or other and bring out a bottle of well-matured Scottish wine. He swallowed a stiff measure but it had no effect on him. He wasn't pretending to be cut up, he was cut up.

'Who do you think is behind it all — Lardvik?'

'No.'

'Why not?'

'No real motive.'

'With all he's going to inherit?'

'It's only a job, the shareholders could sack him to-morrow.'

He wandered around the studio for a while, losing himself among the shadows of the tall steel arc-lamp stands and hanging props.

'Why did you tell me he took those nudes of Ninette?'

He was just passing behind me gripping his whisky glass which was empty. He shrugged his shoulders.

'A joke . . . Ninette and I were great buddies . . . until he came along. It was she who got me in with old Bedlington, he got me out.'

'So he told me.'

'You've spoken to him?' He was surprised.

'I've spoken to everyone. Now tell me, who did take those photographs?'

'A friend of hers.' He was hedging.

'Right now,' I said, and standing up to do so, 'Clementine might be having her throat cut. I've got to know everything!'

'Everything?'

'Just that.'

He took a deep breath, helped himself to another dollop of whisky and faced me without blinking.

'You know Fred Scatz?'

'Yes.'

'You know anything about his background?'

'Most of it.'

'Did you know that he was a thorn in Bedlington's side?'

'Yes.'

'Well, it all starts from there. Bedlington wanted to get rid of Scatz. To do so diplomatically he had to make him slip up. To make him slip up without getting involved himself he had to employ someone to do his dirty work, so he did.'

I offered him a cigarette, lit it for him and glanced once round the studio to make sure that no one else was around among the junk.

'The man he hired was not only in Bedlington's pay, but was in a very strong position. What Bedlington was doing was dirty and anything dirty mustn't be known. This character didn't blackmail old Henry, he just went out with his wife — without him knowing.'

It all sounded good clean fun and I was beginning to regret I didn't have full-time employment at the agency.

'To trip up Fred Scatz this character fed certain pieces of information to me together with a small payroll, and I made sure that the information got into the hands of Cordite Advertising Ltd.'

'You were the go-between?'

'The middle man. This went on for some time. Any parties, on expenses, took place here, and one or two were great fun. This character was handy with a camera and for another small payroll I let him use the studio — but I kept the negatives.'

'For any particular reason?'

'I like naked women. When Bedlington got killed, as I said, I was the last to leave the scene of the crime, but I didn't have anything to do with it.'

'But the man who fed you the information did?'

He put down his glass and took a long pull at his cigarette.

'Maybe.'

'Who was it?'

Slowly he came towards me, stopped, blinked a couple of times and put on a sincere expression.

'Even for Clementine's sake I wouldn't tell you. I might tell the police if they asked, but I wouldn't tell you.'

'Why not?'

'Because I don't know who's paying you, or who you are working for. But I'll help you this much. When we had the odd party Clementine was with me. If you can find her she'll tell you who it is — that should be an incentive for you to find her, mmm?'

I checked the urge to run out of the studio and back home. I had to play it cool, troubled, worried, as though I didn't think she'd ever be found. I managed it quite well, running up the stairs a little too fast, but pausing at the front door to shake his hand long enough to make him feel his secret would never be disclosed.

Out in the mews I walked slowly till I heard the door slam, then I ran like a madman to the main road, grabbed a taxi and told the driver to go to my flat — but quick!

12

Clementine was fast asleep in my double bed when I got in. I didn't undress or turn any sweet music on, but shook her quite hard and told her to sit up.

'What's happened?' She still had a little fear left in her and looked at me with frightened eyes.

'I'm on to something hot . . . I think I know who was responsible for leaking the creative information to Cordite.'

She was hardly interested. Her face was still relaxed and she had a sweet innocent expression around her mouth which made me want to kiss her — but I was a hard business man and didn't spare myself.

'Ever remember going to a party in Everard's studio when Ninette was there?'

'Yes.'

'Do you remember who she was with?'

'Yes.'

'Who?'

'I don't know his name, but he was quite young. Not awfully handsome. Susan was there too — on one occasion.'

'That figures. But you don't know his name, or remember seeing him elsewhere?'

'I've seen him at the studios — Merton Park — on occasions, and at his flat.'

'*His* flat?'

'Yes. Everard and I called on him one night to invite him to a barbecue or something — but he couldn't make it. Funnily enough, now I remember, Susan was there too.'

'Where was the flat?'

'The tower at Notting Hill. You know, that new skyscraper thing that's just been built.'

'Which floor?'

'Couldn't tell you . . . high up though.'

I planted a quick sensational kiss on her beautiful mouth, patted her head and cleared out. The tower block was a quarter of a mile down the road and I wasn't going to waste any time.

★   ★   ★

The wind was blowing furiously as I got out of the cab on the wide pavement outside the Notting Hill Tower. I looked up at the dark looming block of flats which rose eighteen storeys in the night sky with its top-floor lights dotting the dark blue expanse like stars.

I walked into the marbled entrance and looked around for the name board. When I saw it I smiled. There was the name on it of someone I hadn't even got on my suspect list, the name of a young man who was far too busy being an ad.-man for me to consider — Francis Gear, Flat 26, top floor.

Though the lift was very fast it still took a fair time to get to the top. The height, looking out of the windows in the corridor, made one quite giddy, but I didn't stop to enjoy the cheap sensation.

Flat 26 had a letter flap and I carefully pushed it open to see if any light came out of it. There didn't seem to be anyone in but I pressed the bell-push all the same and waited.

In the depths of the apartment something stirred. I couldn't believe that at this time of night a man like Gear would be asleep, but I was wrong. He had been asleep and he wasn't at all pleased to see me. It was, he explained, three o'clock in the morning.

He wore a white towelling arrangement, slippers and a pair of hairy legs. He didn't invite me in but rudely asked me what the hell I wanted.

I had my foot in the door, just in case he felt like slamming it, and I suggested that it might be to our mutual advantage if he saw me for a few minutes.

For quite a while there was a struggle, then, sure that he was hiding something I should find interesting, I charged the door and sent him flying backwards into the flat and gave him a quick one-two in the stomach and on the back of the head. He was out for a good ten minutes.

Running my aching fingers through my hair, I closed the door and switched on the lights.

The flat was snazzy, a really cool hide-out for sexy bachelors. It had everything in it to make a blonde dizzy, even down to the wall of plated glass which gave out onto nothing but a four-hundred-foot drop.

In the small bedroom, furnished with a circular double bed but little else, I found evidence that a blonde had been keeping Mr. Gear company.

The two pillows were still warm and a nylon stocking lay dejectedly abandoned on the floor. She had left her comb on the dresser with a few long strands of golden hair stuck in its teeth.

I had very nearly landed the prize. By now, of course, she had left by the kitchen exit, but a glance out of one of the windows told me how close I had been to ending the whole case. From way up I could see the minute figure of Susan getting into a Mini Minor car. She was in a hell of a hurry and hadn't had the time to dress too well.

I could ring up the police and tell them that my kidnapper was still in London, but they might delay things and anyway Gear was standing in the doorway, now looking nasty and waving an empty wine bottle in my direction.

'Why the rough treatment, Flute? What do you want?'

There was no doubt about it, he was in a menacing mood. Maybe I had disturbed something.

'Susan Trevelyan.'

'What for?'

'Murder.'

Gear was staggered. Playing with a woman was one thing, part of a young executive's duty, but playing with girls who murdered people didn't seem quite fitting. He looked shaken and sat down to think things over.

'You'll have the police round here pretty soon I should imagine,' I said. 'Any idea where she might have gone to?'

'No . . . I didn't even think she'd go.'

I was puzzled and I had to admit it. Gear seemed genuine, he was behaving just like the young executive he was who had been caught out at three in the morning with a blonde in bed who had murdered his boss.

'Just how friendly were you with her?'

'Well, you know . . . I mean . . . she's a nice girl and we were working late and

190

well . . . you know how it is, don't you?'

I knew exactly. Susan had used him to hide from the big chase the police were giving her. I was sufficiently convinced that Gear had just been a weak boy and given in to temptation, but I had a question to ask him all the same.

'You've been to a few of Everard Philbear's parties?'

'Yes.'

'Who with?'

'All sorts of people. Susan sometimes as a matter of fact.'

'Ninette?'

'Mrs. Bedlington?'

'Mrs. Bedlington.'

'Yes. Once.'

'Yet you told me you hardly knew her.'

'She was my boss's wife. I'm not that indiscreet.'

It made sense. There was no reason why he should trust me with any of his secrets.

'The leak. Philbear told me you worked on it under Bedlington's instructions.'

'Did he?'

'Yes.'

'I don't know that he should have.'

'Was it true?'

'Yes. Scatz slows everything down at the agency . . . I thought it a good plan. But Lardvik had quite a lot to do with dishing out information to Cordite you know.'

'Do you think he had anything to do with the murder?'

'You think Susan did, don't you?'

'Yes,' I said, not seeing the connection.

'Did you know he had a daughter?' Gear asked, snapping a lighter under my nose.

'No. But then I didn't know he had a wife.'

'Well, he has a daughter and her mother is Susan Trevelyan.'

I drew on my cigarette and thought for a while. I thought of the photograph I had seen in Susan's flat, the little blonde girl and the sarcastic smile.

'Where is the daughter?' I asked.

'In Sweden with her grandmother — they have more liberal ideas there.'

★　★　★

It was dawn when I left Gear's flat, a little more knowledgeable in the ruthless manners of agency chiefs than I had been, but little else.

Lardvik was up to his neck in trouble. Father of Susan's illegitimate daughter, godfather to Ninette, in the know about the 'leak'. I knew I would have to keep the appointment he had made the night before.

I slumped back to the flat and gazed down at the small shape of the beautiful Clementine asleep on my pillow. I lay down beside her, ran my fingers down her nose and then gave her a passionate kiss to which she responded. I hoped it was me she was dreaming about.

In the morning Francis Gear rang me up. He was concerned by the turn of events and wanted to help all he could. He told me that an unexpected Chamble meeting had been scheduled for ten-thirty and that if I wanted to see Lardvik, as I had intimated the night before, I would have to put my skates on.

Wearing my dark suit, bow tie, white shirt and horn-rimmed glasses, which I always discarded at the front door not having the guts to wear them, I slouched into the Bedlington-Lardvik slaughter house.

I took the lift up to Bedlington's office and found to my surprise that the sudden Chamble meeting was already in progress. Julius himself was sitting behind my half-moon desk with two artists, the advertising manager of Chamble, one of the down-trodden copywriters and Francis Gear, looking like any clean executive should, standing in a circle in front of him.

They were discussing the idea of all going along to the Chamble factory to see a new gimmick which might increase motivational interest in the soap bubbles. They had had staggering sales since the murder had been in the papers and naturally the agency wanted to follow the upward curve with something equally as newsy.

As the others followed Lardvik towards the lift, I slipped away and took to the stairs. Though I wanted to hang on to Lardvik until I got him to answer a few questions, I also had to find out why he wasn't using his office. My mind tended to leap to all sorts of conclusions and I wanted to make sure that Bowels wasn't in there examining another body.

Twelve adult males and five women were sitting on the floor of the regency-striped room giving each other their respective views on a new product which stood in the centre of the floor. It was a motor tyre made of bright green rubber — the committee were deciding whether it would sell to people who owned red cars.

Satisfied why Lardvik hadn't used his own room for the Chamble meeting I headed for the stairs again to join the group.

Down in the street a couple of hired cars waited for us to get in. Without being asked I joined Lardvik and Gear in the front car and smiled at the advertising manager as though we had been introduced but he had forgotten.

On the way this white-haired man explained that they had perfected a new system of manufacturing Chamble — a new formula which would give the bubbles a fresh tingle. The idea was to have a hot bath onto which one sprinkled the new tingling Chamble powder which immediately formed an artificial 'warm' layer of ice. This would have to be broken before getting into the bath, an irresistible attraction to any hygiene-loving Briton. The experiments anyway were in hand and we were going to see them in the laboratory.

The Chamble factory was situated on the North Circular Road. It had a couple of trees outside the entrance, a board a quarter-of-a-mile long telling people what they made and two army surplus searchlights which lit the place up at night in pink. Once inside, one was overpowered by the smell of soap — burning grease and synthetic violet aroma.

After instant coffee in the boardroom we went into the factory, past heavy vats of curdling muck which was quite revolting to look at, through to a clean, sky-lit hangar which was the laboratory. Here a number of men were busy experimenting with Chamble bubbles.

One earnest fellow, with a crew-cut, took us through the whole manufacturing procedure, and I was just getting bored when we reached what he called the 'reverse experiment'. On some ice, in a large container in a refrigerator, he was going to pour an even newer Chamble powder than the one we had heard talked about. The idea of this one was that it should melt the ice, warm up the water and enable anyone to have a hot bath anywhere. So far the powder only heated the water an inch down, but it was a promising beginning.

With a great flourish the man with the crew-cut opened the door of the large refrigerator. In the middle of the ice-room was a large tub, about six foot square; it was brim full of water which had frozen solid.

Interested, everyone found a place round the tub and waited impatiently for crew-cut to wipe away the white frost on the surface of the ice and proceed with the experiment.

With professional aplomb, crew-cut did just that, with a hygienic broom. Then three female assistants screamed, one male physicist fainted and the others just looked aghast.

Embedded deep in the block of ice looking demure and peaceful and very dead was — Susan Trevelyan.

13

I turned round to look at Francis Gear, but he was being led out by two of the assistants. He was feeling sick — maybe he had never seen a frozen girl-friend before, decorated with coagulated blood round the chest where a bullet or knife wound had been inflicted.

The laboratory supervisor was a little agitated but he was soon calmed by the advertising manager who realized, without my assistance as PR, that this was the greatest story yet and that the press would have to be informed before the police.

In an aside I suggested to Lardvik that maybe we should leave the premises and take poor Gear back to his quarters. Though a small puzzle was beginning to buzz around in the back of my mind. How could a dead body be frozen in a matter of a few hours? I had, after all, only seen Susan nine hours earlier leaving the Notting Hill Tower.

Using my status as PR man I exerted my authority and convinced everyone that I had better contacts with the press than anyone else.

Locking myself up in the boardroom, I grabbed the line and dialled Scotland Yard. Chaucer answered and I asked to speak to Bowels. When Bowels had finished his cup of tea he decided to listen to what I had to say.

'Made any big discoveries?' he asked with a laugh in his voice.

'One of about five-foot-seven inches, blonde, blue-eyed, name of Susan Trevelyan,' I said with a laugh in mine.

'You've found her?'

'Yes. Didn't you want me to?'

'Yes . . . yes of course . . . Where is she?' He sounded impressed.

'In a refrigerator at the Chamble factory on the North Circular Road.'

'What is she doing in there?'

'Having a cold bath — like Bedlington.'

I hung up before he could ask me any more questions and then rang up a few of my press pals to whom I had promised a story.

'I've got an idea for one of your columns,' I said to one of them, 'an article about frozen blondes.'

He hung up. Whether he was coming round or was deciding never to speak to me again, I didn't know.

I was certain that Bowels wouldn't care too much about my movements once he had reached the scene of the crime. He knew I was in the clear and I had helped him quite a bit. All I wanted was a few more hours on my own to tie up the loose ends.

Susan had known too much, that was obvious. Either she had unwittingly become involved in the murder of the advertising boss or she had worked for the criminal deliberately. I felt a little bit responsible for her fate, having told a number of people that I knew she was involved. Scatz knew, Everard knew and so, of course, did Lardvik.

As I was leaving the boardroom a couple of police motorcycles revved into the drive outside. Bowels had acted quickly and I heard one of them telling the receptionist in the entrance that they had had orders to seal off the place and let nobody out. Bowels, it seemed, was hoping that the culprit was still hanging around.

I guessed that the Scotland Yard Chief himself would soon be arriving and decided to skip it before that event took place. Using a back entrance just near the washrooms I walked a couple of hundred yards into the next factory area, then crossed the road and walked into the smaller manufacturing premises right opposite Chamble's birthplace.

A dull knitting girl asking me what I wanted, so I asked for Mr. Parkins. She had never heard of Mr. Parkins and I then admitted that perhaps I had made a mistake and could she get me a taxi? To my surprise she obliged and suggested I should take a seat while I waited. I didn't take a seat but stood by the window and watched what was going on at the soap bubble establishment opposite.

Bowels arrived with three other cars and a small black van. He obviously meant business. I also saw Lardvik leaving the premises by a back door and getting into one of the factory's lorries. This intrigued me so much that when my taxi arrived I decided to sit in it a while to see what he was up to.

When the coast was apparently clear of snooping policemen, Lardvik backed the lorry out and put it into gear ready to drive off. But he wasn't too sure about the clutch or something and while he dallied one of the motorcycle boys came out and poked his long nose into the lorry's cabin.

I was amused to see Lardvik all dressed up in the pink overalls of the Chamble drivers, but I stopped smiling when the policeman waved him on. Lardvik had made it and was about to slip away.

Explaining to my driver that I was a private eye on a job, and that if he helped me the reward wasn't to be sneered at, I told him to follow the lorry at a safe distance and not lose it from sight. He was a young man and he took to the chase like a housewife to a new detergent. On several occasions he drew level with Lardvik's lorry forcing me to crouch down on the floor, but eventually the Swede drew up outside St. John's Wood tube station where he got out and took off the overalls.

Abandoning the lorry, he waited by the side of the road wondering whether it would be safer to go by tube or taxi. I told my driver to go and pick him up.

As he saw the taxi approaching Lardvik put out his hand conveniently. It wasn't till he had given Susan's address that I showed myself. I opened the door for him and suggested he should jump in. He looked at me in amazement. He was shocked and very perturbed.

'That was a neat little get-away, Mr. Lardvik, if I may say so,' I said, smiling.

'Yes . . . yes it was.'

'You are frightened of the police?'

'I . . . I have more important things to attend to.'

'In Miss Trevelyan's flat?'

'I don't think it's any of your business.'

Just to make the episode a bit more dramatic I told the driver to head for Scotland Yard. Lardvik froze.

'You can't arrest me,' he protested.

'I have.'

'On what charge?'

'Murder.'

'But whose?'

'Take your choice, Susan or Bedlington, I'm not fussy.'

'You're mad. I know nothing about either of those terrible crimes.'

'Can you prove it?'

'If you give me time.'

'I'll leave the judge to do that. Why were you going to Susan's flat?'

'Collect a few belongings.'

'Evidence?'

'No! I just want to avoid a scandal.'

'I'll help you.'

To Lardvik's surprise I leaned forward and told the cabby to go to the Hammersmith address. We hadn't gone off route and he just touched his cap.

'You have a good motive for getting rid of Miss Trevelyan, of course,' I said, falling back in the seat and lighting myself a cigarette.

'I can't think what.'

'Your daughter.'

He didn't say any more. He had too

many things to think about, like how I had found that out, and why I was always on the spot when he wasn't behaving himself.

The taxi came to a halt outside the block near Hammersmith Bridge and we both got out. I thanked the driver, payed him handsomely and grabbed hold of Lardvik's arm to remind him I meant business.

We climbed the stairs together but I kept well back in case he tried something funny. When we reached the door I wondered how we would get in, but life was full of surprises. He had a key.

'You stayed here with her often?' I asked as he pushed the door open into the familiar hallway.

'No, not often. Our relationship ended some years ago, after the . . . after the trouble.'

'What have you really come for?' I said, kicking the door shut behind me.

'Nothing that will interest you. Personal belongings. I do not wish to be brought into this case if I can possibly help it.'

'Running out on the police won't help you.'

'I was not running out on the police, Mr. Flute, I was getting away from Mr. Gear without him knowing!'

'Gear?'

'Francis Gear.'

The way he said the name told me he was going to explain what he meant. He didn't explain anything at all but went straight to Susan's bedroom and opened the drawer of her dressing-table. Putting his hand right in he pulled out an envelope of fair size and peeped into it. One by one he pulled out some snapshots and handed them to me.

I had seen three of them before, the colour jobs of Ninette in her birthday suit; it was the other six that interested both of us.

Two of them were in black-and-white, ordinary holiday photographs of Susan and Gear hugging each other near some palm trees. They told of three weeks in the sun and everything else that goes with it.

The other four were in Technicolor,

again good photographs, clear, well-composed, an artistic job. They showed Ninette posing on a tiger skin, with a low window behind her overlooking a panoramic view of London, dressed in some flimsy gown which was blowing about in the wind. The detail I thought particularly interesting was her hair. She had dyed it blonde.

I looked at Lardvik but the colour of her hair didn't worry him, he was troubled by the two black-and-white snaps.

'You think Gear's behind it all?' I asked.

'He was obviously friends with both these girls.'

'Taken at his flat,' I said pointing to the ones of Ninette.

'I don't think so. There's Big Ben in the background. Gear doesn't live in a flat with such a view.'

'The Notting Hill Tower?'

'No. These were taken from that new hotel in Knightsbridge.'

I didn't argue. Lardvik was observant and he knew his London.

'How did you know these photographs would be here?' I asked.

'I didn't. Susan always kept her precious secrets in that drawer. I was looking for a photograph of myself, not these.'

'You think these were taken recently?'

'It seems like it. Ninette has never been blonde before.'

Lardvik sat down heavily on the edge of the peacock-blue settee. He was worried about the girls, they had got into trouble and Susan's death was just beginning to make itself felt. His eyes began roaming the room for intimate details, he was in a nostalgic mood and I felt he might start weeping any minute. Quietly I took the photographs from his weak grip and put them in my pocket, then I left the room and Lardvik and the flat. As a suspect he didn't interest me any more, I had higher places to go to.

★　★　★

I reached the Skyscraper Hotel in time to be photographed with a West African minister who was being taken out to dine by an East African minister. Their robes looked warm and comfortable in the thick fog that had suddenly enveloped this particular quarter of London.

In the luxuriously new atmosphere of the hotel I mingled with the crowd of press men and eventually made my way to the reception desk. Behind the counter was a young man, a fly character who was bored to tears by his job.

I slipped a pound note and a photograph of Ninette in a folded visiting card and handed it all to him.

He had seen pictures of nudes before but he was impressed by the money. He glanced to his left at a sergeant-major of a head porter, then handed me back my card.

'Suite sixteen, sir. Seventeenth floor. The lift is to your right.'

On the top floor I found suite sixteen at the end of a bouncy corridor carpeted with rubber foam and Axminster. There was a bell near the door, I rang it.

She opened it herself. She looked pretty with her hair blonde, all silken and bobbing. Her pale lips, her pale complexion, her wide-open eyes with no mascara at all, helped the effect. She was a picture of innocence, possibly spoilt a little by the dry Martini she was holding in one hand and the cigarette she was holding in the other.

She was startled to see me. Before she could say anything, or invite me in, I pushed her backwards into the room and bolted the door behind me.

She recovered her composure quickly enough and just stood there where I had left her while I looked around. There was a bedroom with a bed big enough for twelve people, a bathroom designed to please Neptune and his harem of mermaids, a kitchenette with its own built-in frozen food factory and a sitting-room furnished with plush champagne-coloured fittings and — champagne.

Satisfied that we were alone I turned to face her and smiled. In front of a fireplace with a fitted barbecue there was a tiger skin, and near it a long low window looked over foggy London. Eastwards one would normally have been looking at Big Ben. I had seen the layout before.

'What took you so long?' she asked, making her way to a five-inch-high sofa covered with Eau-de-nil satin.

'I didn't know you wanted me, or I would have come sooner.'

She stared at me for a long time, annoyed by the fact that I had helped myself to one of her cigarettes, a brandy from the cocktail bar, and sat down without being asked.

'Susan Trevelyan was found iced-up in the Chamble factory this morning. I was worried that you might end the same way, but I see you've managed to keep warm.'

I hoped that I was impressing upon her that I wasn't over pleased with her behaviour. She was my client and the least she could have done was let me know where she was.

'Why did you change the colour of your hair?'

Suddenly she remembered she had no make-up on and started getting worried. She put down her glass and got up to go to the bedroom, but I wasn't interested in seeing her all dolled up. Getting up fast I grabbed hold of her small wrist and forced her to sit right down again.

'You're not going anywhere until you've told me why you double-crossed me.'

She was surprised, quite genuinely. Her eyes grew wider and she left her mouth open.

'Double-crossed you? How do you mean? I only came here to hide.'

'Not exactly uncomfortable,' I said, looking around at the gold surroundings.

'The last place you thought of looking. You or anyone else! I was frightened.' She looked it.

'Do you know who killed your husband?'

'No,' she said, her eyes looking even more innocent, her blonde bobbed hair bouncing lazily on her ears as she shook her head.

'Have the police been in contact with you?'

'No, of course not!'

'Who are you hiding from then?'

'Julius Lardvik! I still think he's guilty.' If nothing else this little girl was sticking to her guns, but I thought I'd fire a salvo of my own.

'Who took these?'

I brought out the photographs of herself in the nude and she looked at them without batting an eyelid. All she said, pursing her lips, was, 'They're not very flattering.'

I gave her one of those knowing looks which are supposed to undress women, but as I had a photograph in front of me which was doing the job more effectively it didn't add up to much.

'Here are some more, taken in this very room,' I said. I wanted her to react somehow, but it was impossible. 'Who took them?'

'Everard Philbear,' she admitted after a long time.

'When?'

'Some days ago.'

'Why?'

'You do ask the silliest questions. I was bored! I am bored! It hasn't been much fun staying here all the time you know. There isn't even a decent waiter to tease.'

'How much longer are you going to stay?'

'Till it all blows off.'

'You're joking.'

'Why should I be?'

'None of this will blow off till they find you. Everyone thinks you're dead.'

She stood up and walked over to the fireplace. The electric flames were bright enough to show me her nude silhouette through the thin silken gown she was wearing. I quickly lit another cigarette and tried to compose myself, but the odds were against me. I stood up, crossed the room and joined her.

'I know who killed your husband,' I said, looking deep into her eyes.

She wasn't too interested in him right then but seemed to think that I had something to offer. Just for the hell of it I took her small head in my hands and kissed her feverishly. She had been bored for so long that she pressed her thin body against mine till I had to release her fearing she might break my fountain pen.

'And,' I whispered, 'I can assure you it isn't Lardvik.'

In another passionate embrace I tried to detect a mood of fear, of worry, but she didn't seem to care. Maybe I was going on the wrong track or maybe she had taken a few acting lessons after all.

'Who is it then?' she asked, leading me towards the bedroom.

'I'll come back here and tell you the moment I've had him arrested.'

It took some courage to break away from the feel of her warm limbs, the smell of her heavy scent and the sight of the large double bed in the pink organza room, but I was tough, and I made it.

I reached the door and blew her a kiss. Her eyes were blazing with indignation and I felt that she hated me as much as she had pretended to love me a few seconds before.

'Who *do* you suspect?' She was by my side now. 'I think I have a right to know.'

I looked at her for a long time, held her little pointed chin between my forefinger and thumb and kissed her lightly. 'Everard Philbear, who else?'

I pulled the door open, let myself out and left her all alone to get bored.

When I got to the ground floor of the hotel I found myself a call box and asked for Scotland Yard. The operator was pretty smart and got me through in under eight minutes.

'Bowels,' I said to Bowels, who seemed infuriated that I should have given him the slip again, 'I've found Ninette Bedlington.'

'No! In what sort of condition?'

'Warmish — even hot I'd say.'

'Charred?' His imagination was getting the better of him.

'I wouldn't go that far.'

'Where did you find her?'

'Suite sixteen, the new Skyscraper Hotel.'

'How was it done?'

'What?'

'The murder!'

'I didn't say she was dead, Bowels. She's got blonde hair now, that's all. Probably that's why your men didn't find her. Anyway I'm off to make an arrest. I'll call you if I need you.'

I slammed down the receiver before he could hurt my feelings and left the hotel.

14

He was looking pretty smug sitting behind his desk, until he saw me. I guessed that Ninette had rung him up to say I had gone off at a tangent again, and he wasn't ready for me at all.

Calmly I sat down in the chair opposite him and looked straight in his eyes. It was just on six o'clock and in the corridor I could hear the rest of the staff getting ready to go home.

'What did they do with Susan then?' I asked.

'I don't know. I haven't the time to discuss it now anyway.'

He handed himself a cigarette but he didn't offer me one, so I helped myself from my own packet which made him look real mean.

'I'm just puzzled how you got Susan into that block of ice,' I said with a pleasant smile.

'I don't know what you're talking

about. If that is meant to be a joke I think it's in rather poor taste.'

'No, it's no joke. The police are coming to arrest you for her murder any minute now, so you'd better know what you're talking about.'

Francis Gear looked at me for a long time, very steadily, then he switched on his executive's charm smile.

'What on earth makes you think that I might have had anything to do with all this sordid business?'

'Oh, just a few clues here and there — the odd bit of imaginative thinking.'

'You're accusing me of killing Susan?'

'Yes.'

'Hadn't you better be careful what you say — I might sue you.'

'You might.'

We both smoked our cigarettes as calmly as we could. I was waiting for him to say something, and he was waiting for me to start. We both waited; it became a battle of wits, who would crack up first. I didn't have anything to worry about and my opponent was a good deal weaker than I had suspected. After only a minute he spoke.

'You really think I had something to do with the murder?'

'I don't think — I know.'

Luckily he had finished his cigarette quickly and he was able to stub most of it out as he leaned forward to give me one of those murderous looks people give you when you accuse them of being murderers.

'What *do* you know, Flute?'

'I know that the blonde who escaped from your flat last night was Ninette Bedlington and that she rang you up about ten minutes ago from her suite at the Skyscraper Hotel to tell you that I suspected Everard Philbear.'

Francis Gear, who till then had been the epitome of British calmness, was getting rattled. He was still stubbing out his cigarette and thinking hard what he should say next.

'Would you like me to call one of the copywriters to help you make up a good story?' I asked. I couldn't think of a better insult.

'All right! So you know a bit about me

and Ninette. That doesn't prove any-thing!'

'It proves that you lied to me in the beginning and that you'll lie some more.'

He was breaking. He was standing up now and pacing the small room like a good executive should.

'I'll be quite frank with you,' he went on. 'When Henry died, Ninette rather threw herself on me . . . she needed the company.'

'Oh that won't do,' I said, taking the photographs out of my pocket. 'I can trace your friendship with her much farther back than that.'

I watched him pick up the set of photographs. He didn't look long at the ones of Ninette — the two of himself with Susan caused him some anxiety though.

'Where did you get these?'

'Why should I tell you?'

'Where did you get them?'

He was in a bad mood. His eyebrows were nearly meeting above his nose and he looked dangerous. I uncrossed my legs and re-crossed them. In my new position I could kick him with my right foot if he came at me.

'What is more interesting, surely, is where did Susan get those colour shots of Ninette? They were the ones that turned her against you, weren't they?'

I was working on a dead certain hunch. I didn't yet know how Gear had got involved in Bedlington's killing, but that he was involved I was sure. In an attempt to clear his name he had asked Susan, an old flame, to help him, then she had found out that he was friendly with Ninette and had threatened to give the story away.

'Let's start at the beginning, Gear, shall we? Or would you rather start at the end, when I pick up this receiver and dial 999?'

To impress him that I meant business I picked up the telephone and started dialling.

His reaction, for a man who hadn't yet been proved guilty, was violent. Unexpectedly he lashed out at me and sent me flying backwards — even my right foot didn't have time to come into action.

As I tried to get up, he grabbed hold of

my lapels and mercilessly struck me in the face. It was a powerful and well-aimed punch and for quite a while I lay dazed in the corner of the office. As soon as I could, I got to my feet, but a little late.

He had made a clean get-away and was now halfway down the corridor shouting for help. Two secretaries with honeycomb nests on their heads rushed in to assist me and fussed long enough to give Gear more leeway.

Not for the first time in my life I gave proof that when circumstances necessitated it I could be ungentlemanly. Taking both the secretary birds' heads I banged them together and left them with a couple of good headaches and screams of confusion.

I didn't wait for the lift to come up but hurled myself down the stairs. Out in the street there was no sign of Gear. I wasn't surprised, he might have hidden any-where. I hailed a taxi, jumped in and tried to convince the driver that I was in sufficient a hurry for him to risk turning round in a one-way street and heading for Notting Hill Gate come fair or foul. But he was an old man with thoughts of his pension and after lighting his pipe he quietly drove down Park Lane, round the corner and up into the Park.

Nursing the side of my jaw I decided to relax while I had the chance. I knew that I might well have to have a reserve of energy when I got to the tower flats.

When we got there I gave the old man his fare, ran into the large carpeted entrance hall and managed to slip by the hall porter unnoticed and up the stairs to the first floor where I got into the lift. I shot up to the eighteenth storey and got out.

It was all beginning to make sense now. Francis Gear was no doubt a genius at exploiting others but he also had a cranky thing about heights. Looking through the corridor window I could see the whole of London lit up below me, a beautiful sight but one I still didn't have the time to admire.

There was no one about and I went straight to his door and rang the buzzer. As might have been expected there was no answer, so I walked along to another door which led to the tradesmen's lift and back stairs. The kitchen door of the flat had a window, and through it I watched Gear gulp down a glass of milk with some glucose tablets. He was really getting ready for a tough time.

He looked up suddenly, saw me, picked up the milk bottle to hurl it in my direction — then hesitated. I was trying the door handle and it was working.

'Look, Gear,' I said, walking into the blue-and-white cooking room. 'All I want you to do is come to the station with me.'

'Why?'

The milk he had been drinking had left a shadow of white moisture round his upper lip and it made him look sick.

'To answer a few questions, clear your name.'

'All right.'

He was a defeated man. His hands went limp at his sides when he put down the milk bottle, but they were as ready as a cowboy's itching to handle a gun, and push a bullet through my old belly. His acting was improving and I didn't trust him at all.

'Can I get my coat?'

'Of course.'

He didn't try anything funny, he just turned round slowly and walked into the living-room, and I followed him.

I was ready for her, of course. As soon as I had passed through the door I dropped to my knees and the iron bar she was going to sap me with caught me between the shoulder blades. I rolled over quickly and got to my feet fast.

Ninette was surprised. In fact she was paralysed, not by my agility but by the fact that Gear was now holding a small Colt in his right hand.

He was aiming it at me, but couldn't hold it as steadily as Susan had held her Mauser. Timing was all that it required and I took a chance.

I threw myself at Gear across the room and over the back of the sofa. I hit his stomach with my head and managed to grip the barrel of the gun. If he fired most of my fingers would be blown off, but he didn't fire — the safety catch hadn't been released.

We wrestled for about three seconds, then I got the better of him and pulled the gun out of his hand. I didn't wait for him to retaliate but darted back across the room to where Ninette was standing and got behind her. She struggled for a while but I managed to pin her elbows behind her. The whole operation had been as quick as it had been dangerous, and I was aware that a grin was splitting my face in two.

Gear was now crouching behind a tall-backed armchair and behind him was the sheet-glass window. It was a stalemate. If I fired I wouldn't hit him, and only waste what ammunition there was, so instead I acted like any gentleman would.

'I'll shoot her if you don't stand up, Gear!' I shouted.

'See if I care!'

Ninette reacted. She was scared. Something had turned the tables and they didn't seem to be friends any more. But then maybe it was all an act. Just to be helpful she started struggling and managed to push my gun off the target and in that instant Gear made a dive for the bedroom.

I got Ninette under control again but realized it was too late. Any minute now the fight I had been expecting would start.

He didn't choose the handiest of weapons, just a twelve-bore, double-barrelled shotgun, which might possibly damage my face if I got within a hundred yards of it. He was poking the gun round from behind the bedroom door and I knew that he had it over me. If I shot at him I wouldn't be certain of hitting the target. If he pulled the trigger it would take the daily woman a fair time to mop up the blood off the walls.

Using more gentlemanly tactics I held Ninette right in front of me and shouted a few encouraging words to Gear.

'If you fire you'll hit her!'

'Big deal!'

It was Ninette who pulled me down to the ground. She knew her man. She knew when he meant business, and fear gave her the strength of three men. As Gear fired, I was pulled over her back and down. The lead peppered the whole room, spattering the giant sheet-window and pock-marking it for life. The second volley was shot at random through the oily cloud of smoke and then I knew I had him.

Ninette, if she was hurt, said nothing, but lay in a faint on the floor. The backs of my legs felt rough and I guessed by the uncomfortable feeling in my left arm that some of the shot had hit me, but this was no time to be sentimental about one's limbs.

I fired at point blank range into the bedroom as I advanced, and then caught the full power of the gun butt as it hit me across the neck. Using all the instinctive judo tactics at my command, I dropped the Colt, grabbed hold of his gun and pulled it towards me. Catching Gear off balance I swung him over my right shoulder but failed to let go. We both crashed to the floor and rolled over into the living-room.

A searing pain gripped my knee and I tried to twist round as I felt my leg being snapped off. I kicked out and caught

Gear in the small of the back. He let out an agonized groan, so I kicked out again.

He got to his knees and was gripping his stomach as I twisted round to lie on my back. Never two without three, I thought, and kicked out again, catching the edge of his chin with my heel. This smack sent him reeling back against the wall of glass. His head hit it with full force and a whistling snap cracked the air as the sheet-window split in half.

Ninette screamed and I looked up. Horrified, I saw the glass disintegrate into millions of fractured pieces. Gear lost his balance and fell backwards tearing at the open space behind him. In a second he was gone, falling into the terrible emptiness of the night.

The blood-curdling scream stopped when he hit the roofs of the houses below, and only the sickening thump of his body as it bounced off onto the pavement confirmed that he was dead.

★ ★ ★

If Ninette looked beautiful when she was pale, she had never looked more beautiful in her life before. She was a brave girl who had never reckoned on being in such circumstances. Brave and bad and agile because she had crossed the room to pick up the Colt before I could fully recover from what had just happened.

Till that moment I had never really suspected her of having actually committed the crimes, but now I could see quite clearly that she was the guilty party.

But I was wrong again. With a trusting smile she handed me the gun, butt first, and I had to get used to the idea of having to work out who had done what and why.

I watched her move across the room to the dusty telephone and pick up the receiver. With trembling finger she found the 'nine' on the dial and started moving it. Quickly I crossed the room and gently wrestled the receiver out of her hand and replaced it on the cradle.

'There's no need to call the police or the ambulance people, someone will have done that already. What you must do is work out exactly what you are going to tell Mr. Bowels when he starts asking you questions. Some of the facts might best be kept from his twisted mind, mmm? Besides, I think I ought to know your life story first.'

15

I lit Ninette a cigarette and suggested we should move to the bedroom. I had no ulterior motives but the sitting-room, with its shattered glass wall, was getting remarkably draughty, it was beginning to rain and the sounds coming from the street below of crowds gathering to examine Gear's crumpled body were a trifle disturbing.

'Did you want to lie down?' Ninette asked, stretching herself like a cat on the double bed.

'All I want to do is hear the truth, the whole truth and nothing but,' I said sitting on a hard chair in the farthest corner of the room. Ninette was becoming increasingly appealing.

'The whole story is very simple if a little sordid,' she said.

'Murders usually are.'

'Francis and I were lovers. Henry found out and Francis killed him.'

'Just like that?'

'Very nearly. It wasn't premeditated, it was an accident, and all I did in the whole affair was try to save Francis from being accused.'

'An accessory after the fact?'

'I suppose so.'

'Can you fill in a bit more of the background?'

She took the spare pillow from the place in the bed where Francis usually slept, and slipped it behind her own; she was propped up comfortably now, smoking, even smiling. She was an odd customer.

'I wasn't very fond of Henry. Our marriage was fun at first because I wasn't used to all that money; after six months I got bored.'

'That's a new angle on marriage.'

'He seldom entertained at home, and when he did it was to talk shop without being disturbed. One day he brought Francis back, and the shop they talked about was a bit underhand.'

'The chopping of Scatz?'

'Yes. I'd been faithful to Henry till

then, but when I realized what sort of bastard he was I let myself be attracted to Francis.'

'Without too much difficulty.'

'He wasn't any great shakes.'

I sighed for her. She would never be satisfied, she was that sort, but I liked looking at her, I had no grumbles at all.

'How did Gear do it, the killing?'

'I wasn't there.'

'But he told you about it?'

'Oh yes, he told me about it. It was all my fault you see, I was careless once or twice and Henry found out about Francis and me. He accused me outright of being unfaithful and I didn't deny it. He said he was going to get a divorce and cite Francis so I told him to go right ahead. Everything would then have followed its normal course if Clementine hadn't showed up!'

'I wondered where she fitted in.'

Business being business and the high pressure of advertising completely numbing men's normal senses, Francis and Henry Bedlington had apparently continued to work together quite happily on the urgent Chamble campaign as though nothing had happened. The situation was a tricky one, for Bedlington anyway, as he had hired Gear's services to leak the creative information to Cordite on Scatz's behalf and was a bit in his debt. However, copy was written, television scripts were drafted, layouts poured out of the studios and photographic session followed photographic session. It was during one of these, when Clementine was stripping to get into the bubble bath, that Gear noticed a look in Henry's eye.

When, the following day, he went into the studio and found them locked in each other's arms, Henry dressed, Clementine not, Francis suggested in no uncertain terms that perhaps divorce proceedings should be dropped. But poor Francis didn't know Henry.

'They had an argument?'

'Just a little one. Henry told Francis to get the hell out of it, Francis refused, so Henry gave him the sack! By this time, darling Clementine had escaped from the scene carrying her clothes and, so Francis told me, within seconds they came to blows.'

'Henry and Gear?'

'Yes. Poor Francis didn't remember how it happened, but after a struggle, during which both men went white with rage, he found Henry lying on the floor with a polythene bag over his head . . . dead.'

'Asphyxiated?'

Ninette nodded her head. For a moment I imagined I saw a tear in her left eye, but I decided that this was wishful thinking.

'What happened when he realized he'd killed your husband?'

'He lost his head. He left the studio — luckily locking it and keeping the key — and went straight to Susan.'

'Why her?'

'Susan and he were very dear friends — before I came along.'

'I see,' I said. 'What did Susan do?'

'Francis knew that Susan was in love with him, he also knew that she hoped they would get married, so he spilled her a big story about being terrified of the police, underlining the fact that if they even found him only guilty of manslaughter their plans would be ruined. Susan pulled out all the stops to save her man.'

'She did?'

'She was an intelligent girl and knew her way around. She gave Francis a stiff drink, told him to pull himself together and think big. He was an ad. man, had imagination, he had hoodwinked the public for years telling them to buy a lot of rubbish, it would be a simple matter for him to spin the police a good story. Francis knew that by incriminating someone else, it would give him time to get an alibi. It was Susan who thought of getting you to muddle things up.'

Women were strange creatures. I couldn't help remembering the happy cup of coffee I had enjoyed at the blonde's flat. She had been so kind to me, so thoughtful, so loving — yet she must have been planning my destruction all the time.

'Why did she pick me out?' I asked, interested.

'Francis knew about you, he knew you

were no PR man, he knew you were involved in the leak, that Bedlington had brought you in and only told you half the story — you were a cinch! What better to get the police's back up and muddle things than a private 'tec?'

I had a sour taste in my mouth and badly felt like a drink, so I left the pretty girl lying on the bed for a minute and hunted around for a drop of something. In the sitting-room a gale was blowing bits of plaster all over the place. I found a bottle of gin and two glasses and picked up the water jug, but it fell to pieces in my hand cracked by the shot from the 12-bore.

'Who rang me up — Susan?'

'I believe so.'

I was back in the bedroom and handing Ninette a good measure.

'And who locked me in the studio?'

'One of them. They watched all your movements till you got out.'

'Then what?'

'Francis went back on the scene of the crime and took Henry's ring.'

'After ringing up the police who were

supposed to find me with the dead body.'

'Yes.'

'Why did he take the ring particularly?'

'He had seen Clementine wearing it and she had had a row with Bedlington which everyone knew about; he thought she might be a good suspect as far as you were concerned. Now that you'd got away it was obvious you'd try to find out who had locked you in, at least.'

The gin didn't taste so good by itself so I got up from my hard chair and padded into the kitchen. In the fridge I found a couple of bottles of tonic; no one had shot them, so I took them back to the bedroom with an opener.

'How did Gear get the ring to you?' I asked sitting on the edge of the bed.

'He brought it himself. He had convinced Susan that it was best if they parted and went around to see as many friends as possible and plant alibis.'

'Was it his idea that you should ring me up?'

'I was the one person who could help him. For me to ask a private detective to find a missing husband would seem normal. When he handed me the ring I realized I could spin you a good story.'

'You then intended me to get round to Clementine?'

'Why not? She was the most likely person to have a motive, and that's what you people always look for.'

'You tried hard enough to get Lardvik incriminated though,' I said. I was beginning to find it hard to hide my vexation. I had been taken for the ride of my life all along the way.

'The more the merrier. We wanted to muddle things up, that was all.'

An ambulance bell in the street below was waking up everyone in the district. The odd shout, the revving of engines indicated that we wouldn't be left alone long.

'You underrated me a bit, didn't you?' I asked. I was fishing for compliments, I had been good about that for too long.

She didn't answer. The fact was that if I hadn't been brought into the story she would not have got into the jam she was in now.

'I suppose it was Francis or Susan who

241

put the polythene bag in my coat pocket to make things tougher for me with the police?'

'I expect so.'

'And those photographs of you in the nude — Gear took them, not Everard Philbear?'

She had never blushed in my presence before, but now she did. Her legs were crossed and she uncrossed them to tuck them under her skirt. She still looked lovely leaning against the pillows of the vast bed.

'Yes,' she said after a while.

'Why?'

She shrugged her shoulders and pouted. I knew why. She had a nice little figure, a good complexion, she wanted to be admired. Her husband had stopped her going on stage to be admired publicly so she had decided to be admired in private. There was nothing wrong, nothing wrong at all.

'What made you decide to hide?' I asked.

'Francis. We were in love, he thought so anyway, he had killed my husband, the least I could do was stay with him so that he had someone to talk to when he came back from the office.'

'You hid at the hotel all the time?'

'I occasionally came here.'

'Why was it necessary to kidnap Clementine?'

Ninette let out a long sigh and shrugged her shoulders. 'Susan's idea! The whole trouble was that two teams were covering up for Francis, me not doing very much but keeping him morally uplifted and Susan doing a lot. Clementine knew too much, she knew I was friends with Francis anyway; and worse, she knew Everard who could have told her all about us.'

'Who broke into her flat and tried to frighten her?'

'Susan. It didn't work because you started nosing around, so they kidnapped her — killing two birds with one stone, getting her out of the way and making the police suspicious of her.'

'Why was I taken for a ride then?'

'You got in the way and Francis honestly thought that you could be bought. He intended having a long chat with you — but you got away.'

I glanced at my watch, it was getting late and the police were taking their time getting to the flat. I was beginning to wonder what steps I should take, but I didn't know the whole story yet. I could guess the bits Ninette hadn't told me, like the way Susan had cleverly led me to believe that Lardvik had been in the flat the night I was sapped, when it was actually Gear, and that it was Lardvik who had left the threatening notes in the bath, but I wasn't sure who had killed her. Ninette had a motive, Susan and she were rivals.

'Who killed Susan?'

'Francis.'

'Why?'

'She found out about us. Everard must have given her the latest photographs or something. She threatened to tell the police everything unless Francis left the country with her. She couldn't be trusted.'

'How did Gear kill her?'

'I don't know.'

'How did he get her to the Chamble factory?'

'They were there — some business reason, they were always going there on business. He probably shot her and then put her in the bath.'

It figured. He had disposed of one body that way, why not another.

'When he had got rid of Susan he came here, and you were waiting for him?'

Ninette nodded. She was now aware that she was lying on a dead man's bed in a dead man's flat. The thought began to haunt her and she moved to the edge to get up.

'I didn't know he had killed Susan, not until tonight. I never thought he'd go to such lengths . . . I would have stopped him. I was in danger myself even.'

Maybe she wasn't acting. I couldn't tell any more. She was looking down at the floor now and her hands had begun trembling.

'Had you any plans of escape?'

She looked up and smiled. She even laughed. She laughed a little too long and a little too obviously. She was sick.

'Yes, we had plans. We were going to Australia! Me in the outback, can you imagine it! He had big plans, he was going to start his own agency out there and I was going to model. That's why he took those photographs at the hotel.'

'He really didn't think he'd be found out?'

'He didn't consider himself guilty. It was an accident and he had got involved. Everything happened so quickly.'

Somewhere in the sitting-room behind me I heard a noise, but I didn't move. Ninette hadn't heard it, so I asked her another question.

'Has Lardvik been involved in any of this?'

'Not knowingly. Poor man, he's always been so kind to me, took his duties as a godfather very seriously. He thought that introducing me to Henry was the best present he had ever made me. It must have been a shock.'

'He was a bit tied up with Susan,' I said.

'That was all over. He's been a bit

unlucky with his women friends hasn't he?'

She was sitting cross-legged on the edge of the bed finishing her cigarette. Her small chin rested on her clasped hand and her eyes looked straight ahead at nothing.

'What will happen to me?'

'Depends on your lawyer.'

'And the evidence we produce in court!' A deep voice said behind me.

Bowels was standing in the doorway with Chaucer beside him and a couple of policemen.

'You have a warrant for her arrest?' I turned round slowly to impress upon him that he hadn't surprised me even if Ninette had jumped out of her skin.

Bowels, however, was in one of his kinder moods and he asked the 'good lady' if she would be kind enough to accompany him to the station to answer a few questions concerning the gentleman who had unintentionally stepped out for a walk.

I didn't ask the detectives how long they had been there but my guess was that they had heard a good deal of Ninette's confession. Though she was pretty deeply involved and the whole business had been nasty, with luck the law wouldn't put her away for too long.

Bowels made way for Ninette as she got up and walked bravely out of the room and he waited for me to follow before sealing off the flat.

Unlike me he had a whole set routine to go through before closing the case, but as far as I was concerned this was the end of the line, or nearly.

* * *

My car was parked outside the block of flats in Bayswater Road and a policeman was standing by it. He didn't say anything till I questioned him about it, then he told me that it had been found abandoned just off the North Circular Road near the Chamble factory. Detective Inspector Bowels had given instructions for it to be returned, he told me, and I thanked him but didn't give him a tip.

Upstairs in the cool luxury of the flat I

had every intention of having a quiet dinner with Clementine and then going to bed — but this was not to be. Uncle Leopold had returned and had taken a liking to my female friend.

He was annoyed that I should interrupt his *tête-à-tête* and began a long explanation about how he had got terribly mixed up with a funny old woman who had fallen head over heels in love with him. He hadn't, till then, he admitted, thought of himself as a Don Juan, but it was quite obvious by what she had said that he had charm in abundance.

I sat opposite the television set and switched it on. Uncle was holding Clementine's hand and talking ten to the dozen. The only thing that would make him shut up was the bright light of the square box. A newscaster came on and smiled at the three of us; after telling us something awful about the Common Market he said, 'Francis Gear, the young advertising executive who worked for Henry Bedlington murdered eleven days ago, was found dead outside his block of flats this evening. The police were to charge him with the murder of Henry Bedlington to-morrow.'

Clementine was looking at me with astonishment, and was about to ask a few questions, but Uncle Leo stopped her.

'Stop fidgeting, my darling, and listen to the cricket scores, they're doing wonders in India!'

THE END